KIM STANLEY ROBINSON

Winner of the Hugo and Nebula awards
World Fantasy award
Locus award
John W. Campbell award

"Simply one of our best writers."
— *Gene Wolfe*

"One of the finest short story writers around."
— *Locus*

"A powerful and consistent fiction voice."
— *New York Times*

"Robinson's writing ranks in the highest levels ..."
— *Publishers Weekly*

"It's no coincidence that one of our most visionary science fiction writers is also a profoundly good nature writer."
— *Los Angeles Times*

"The best nature writer in the U.S. today also happens to write science fiction."
— *The Ends of the Earth*

"The foremost writer of literary utopias."
— *Time*

THE LUCKY STRIKE

plus

A Sensitive Dependence on
Initial Conditions

and

"A Real Joy to be Had"
Outspoken Interview

KIM STANLEY ROBINSON

PM PRESS | 2009

Kim Stanley Robinson © 2009
This edition © 2009 PM Press

First published:
"The Lucky Strike"
Universe 14 (ed. Terry Carr), Doubleday, 1984.

"A Sensitive Dependence on Initial Conditions"
Author's Choice #20, Pulphouse, 1991.

ISBN: 978-1-60486-085-6
LCCN: 2009901381

PM Press
P.O. Box 23912
Oakland, CA 94623
PMPress.org

Printed in the USA on recycled paper.

Cover: John Yates/Stealworks.com
Inside design: Josh MacPhee/Justseeds.org

CONTENTS

THE LUCKY STRIKE

WAR BREEDS STRANGE PASTIMES. In July of 1945 on Tinian island in the North Pacific, Captain Frank January had taken to piling pebble cairns on the crown of Mount Lasso—one pebble for each B-29 take-off, one cairn for each mission. The largest cairn had four hundred stones in it. It was a mindless pastime, but so was poker. The men of the 509th had played a million hands of poker, sitting in the shade of a palm around an upturned crate sweating in their skivvies, swearing and betting all their pay and cigarettes, playing hand after hand after hand, until the cards got so soft and dog-eared you could have used them for toilet paper. Captain January had gotten sick of it, and after he lit out for the hilltop a few times some of his crewmates started trailing him. When their pilot Jim Fitch joined them it became an official pastime, like throwing flares into the compound or going hunting for stray Japs. What Captain January thought of the development he didn't say. The others grouped near Captain Fitch, who passed around his battered flask. "Hey, January," Fitch called. "Come on, have a shot."

January wandered over and took the flask. Fitch laughed at his pebble. "Practicing your bombing up here, eh, Professor?"

"Yah," January said sullenly. Anyone who read more than the funnies was Professor to Fitch. Thirstily January knocked back some rum. He could drink it any way he pleased up here, out from under the eye of the group psychiatrist. He passed the flask on to Lieutenant Matthews, their navigator.

"That's why he's the best," Matthews joked. "Always practicing."

Fitch laughed. "He's best because I make him be best, right, Professor?"

January frowned. Fitch was a bulky youth, thick-featured, pig-eyed—a thug, in January's opinion. The rest of the crew were all in their mid-twenties like Fitch, and they liked the captain's bossy roughhouse style. January, who was thirty-seven, didn't go for it. He wandered away, back to the cairn he had been building. From Mount Lasso they had an overview of the whole island, from the harbor at Wall Street to the north field in Harlem. January had observed hundreds of B-29s roar off the four parallel runways of the north field and head for Japan. The last quartet of this particular mission buzzed across the width of the island, and January dropped four more pebbles, aiming for crevices in the pile. One of them stuck nicely.

"There they are!" said Matthews. "They're on the taxiing strip."

January located the 509th's first plane. Today, the first of August, there was something more interesting to watch than the usual Superfortress parade. Word was out that General Le May wanted to take the 509th's mission away from it. Their commander Colonel Tibbets had gone and bitched to La May in person, and the general had agreed the mission was theirs, but on one condition: one of the general's men was to make a test flight with the 509th, to make sure they were fit for combat over Japan. The general's man had arrived, and now he was down there in the strike plane, with Tibbets and the whole first team. January sidled back to his mates to view the takeoff with them.

"Why don't the strike plane have a name, though?" Haddock was saying.

Fitch said, "Lewis won't give it a name because it's not his plane, and he knows it." The others laughed. Lewis and his crew were naturally unpopular, being Tibbets' favorites.

"What do you think he'll do to the general's man?" Matthews asked.

The others laughed at the very idea. "He'll kill an engine at takeoff, I bet you anything," Fitch said. He pointed at the wrecked B-29s that marked the end of every runway, planes whose engines had given out on takeoff. "He'll want to show that he wouldn't go down if it happened to him."

"'Course he wouldn't!" Matthews said.

"You hope," January said under his breath.

"They let those Wright engines out too soon," Haddock said seriously. "They keep busting under the takeoff load."

"Won't matter to the old bull," Matthews said. Then they all started in about Tibbets' flying ability, even Fitch. They all thought Tibbets was the greatest. January, on the other hand, liked Tibbets even less than he liked Fitch. That had started right after he was assigned to the 509th. He had been told he was part of the most important group in the war, and then given a leave. In

Vicksburg a couple of fliers just back from England had bought him a lot of whiskies, and since January had spent several months stationed near London they had talked for a good long time and gotten pretty drunk. The two were really curious about what January was up to now, but he had stayed vague on it and kept returning the talk to the blitz. He had been seeing an English nurse, for instance, whose flat had been bombed, family and neighbors killed … But they had really wanted to know. So he had told them he was onto something special, and they had flipped out their badges and told him they were Army Intelligence, and that if he ever broke security like that again he'd be transferred to Alaska. It was a dirty trick. January had gone back to Wendover and told Tibbets so to his face, and Tibbets had turned red and threatened him some more. January despised him for that. The upshot was that January was effectively out of the war, because Tibbets really played his favorites. January wasn't sure he really minded, but during their year's training he had bombed better than ever, as a way of showing the old bull he was wrong to write January off. Every time their eyes had met it was clear what was going on. But Tibbets never backed off no matter how precise January's bombing got. Just thinking about it was enough to cause January to line up a pebble over an ant and drop it.

"Will you cut that out?" Fitch complained. "I swear you must hang from the ceiling when you take a shit so you can practice aiming for the toilet." The men laughed.

"Don't I bunk over you?" January asked. Then he pointed. "They're going."

Tibbets' plane had taxied to runway Baker. Fitch passed the flask around again. The tropical sun beat on them, and the ocean surrounding the island blazed white. January put up a sweaty hand to aid the bill of his baseball cap.

The four props cut in hard, and the sleek Superfortress quickly trundled up to speed and roared down Baker. Three-quarters of the way down the strip the outside right prop feathered.

"Yow!" Fitch crowed. "I told you he'd do it!"

The plane nosed off the ground and slewed right, then pulled back on course to cheers from the four young men around January. January pointed again. "He's cut number three, too."

The inside right prop feathered, and now the plane was pulled up by the left wing only, while the two right props windmilled uselessly. "Holy smoke!" Haddock cried. "Ain't the old bull something?"

They whooped to see the plane's power, and Tibbets' nervy arrogance.

"By God, La May's man will remember this flight," Fitch hooted. "Why, look at that! He's banking!"

Apparently taking off on two engines wasn't enough for Tibbets; he banked the plane right until it was standing on its dead wing, and it curved back toward Tinian.

Then the inside left engine feathered.

War tears at the imagination. For three years Frank January had kept his imagination trapped, refusing to give it any play whatsoever. The dangers threatening him, the effects of the bombs, the fate of the other participants in the war, he had refused to think about any of it. But the war tore at his control. That English nurse's flat. The missions over the Ruhr. The bomber just below him blown apart by flak. And then there had been a year in Utah, and the viselike grip that he had once kept on his imagination had slipped away.

So when he saw the number two prop feather, his heart gave a little jump against his sternum and helplessly he was up there with Ferebee, the first team bombardier. He would be looking over the pilots' shoulders….

"Only one engine?" Fitch said.

"That one's for real," January said harshly. Despite himself he *saw* the panic in the cockpit, the frantic rush to power the two right engines. The plane was dropping fast and Tibbets leveled it off, leaving them on a course back toward the island. The two right props spun, blurred to a shimmer. January held his breath. They needed more lift; Tibbets was trying to pull it over the island. Maybe he was trying for the short runway on the south half of the island.

But Tinian was too tall, the plane too heavy. It roared right into the jungle above the beach, where 42nd Street met their East River. It exploded in a bloom of fire. By the time the sound of the explosion struck them they knew no one in the plane had survived.

Black smoke towered into white sky. In the shocked silence on Mount Lasso insects buzzed and creaked. The air left January's lungs with a gulp. He had been with Ferebee there at the end, he had heard the desperate shouts, seen the last green rush, been stunned by the dentist-drill-all-over pain of the impact.

"Oh my God," Fitch was saying. "Oh my God." Matthews was sitting. January picked up the flask, tossed it at Fitch.

"C-come on," he stuttered. He hadn't stuttered since he was sixteen. He led the others in a rush down the hill. When they got to Broadway a jeep careened toward them and skidded to a halt. It was Colonel Scholes, the old bull's exec. "What happened?"

Fitch told him.

"Those damned Wrights," Scholes said as the men piled in. This time one had failed at just the wrong moment; some welder stateside had kept flame to metal a second less than usual—or something equally minor, equally trivial—and that had made all the difference.

They left the jeep at 42nd and Broadway and hiked east over a narrow track to the shore. A fairly large circle of trees was burning. The fire trucks were already there.

Scholes stood beside January, his expression bleak. "That was the whole first team," he said.

"I know," said January. He was still in shock, in imagination crushed, incinerated, destroyed. Once as a kid he had tied sheets to his arms and waist, jumped off the roof and landed right on his chest; this felt like that had. He had no way of knowing what would come of this crash, but he had a suspicion that he had indeed smacked into something hard.

Scholes shook his head. A half hour had passed, the fire was nearly out. January's four mates were over chattering with the Seabees. "He was going to name the plane after his mother," Scholes said to the ground. "He told me that just this morning. He was going to call it *Enola Gay*."

At NIGHT THE JUNGLE breathed, and its hot wet breath washed over the 509th's compound. January stood in the doorway of his Quonset barracks hoping for a real breeze. No poker tonight. Voices were hushed, faces solemn. Some of the men had helped box up the dead crew's gear. Now most lay on their bunks. January gave up on the breeze, climbed onto his top bunk to stare at the ceiling.

He observed the corrugated arch over him. Cricketsong sawed through his thoughts. Below him a rapid conversation was being carried on in guilty undertones, Fitch at its center.

"January is the best bombardier left," he said. "And I'm as good as Lewis was."

"But so is Sweeney," Matthews said. "And he's in with Scholes."

They were figuring out who would take over the strike. January scowled. Tibbets and the rest were less than twelve hours dead, and they were squabbling over who would replace them.

January grabbed a shirt, rolled off his bunk, put the shirt on.

"Hey, Professor," Fitch said. "Where you going?"

"Out."

Though midnight was near it was still sweltering. Crickets shut up as he walked by, started again behind him. He lit a cigarette. In the dark the MPs patrolling their fenced-in compound were like pairs of walking armbands. The 509th, prisoners in their own army. Fliers from other groups had taken to throwing rocks over the fence. Forcefully January expelled smoke, as if he could expel his disgust with it. They were only kids, he told himself. Their minds had been shaped in the war, by the war, and for the war. They knew you couldn't mourn the dead for long; carry around a load like that and your own engines might fail. That was all right with January. It was an attitude that Tibbets had helped to form, so it was what he deserved. Tibbets would *want* to be forgotten in favor of the mission, all he had lived for was to drop the gimmick on the Japs, he was oblivious to anything else, men, wife, family, anything.

So it wasn't the lack of feeling in his mates that bothered January. And it was natural of them to want to fly the strike they had been training a year for. Natural, that is, if you were a kid with a mind shaped by fanatics like Tibbets, shaped to take orders and never imagine consequences. But January was not a kid, and he wasn't going to let men like Tibbets do a thing to his mind. And the gimmick … the gimmick was not natural. A chemical bomb of some sort, he guessed. Against the Geneva Convention. He stubbed his cigarette against the sole of his sneaker, tossed the butt over the fence. The tropical night breathed over him. He had a headache.

For months now he had been sure he would never fly a strike. The dislike Tibbets and he had exchanged in their looks (January was acutely aware of looks) had been real and strong. Tibbets had understood that January's record of pinpoint accuracy in the runs over the Salton Sea had been a way of showing contempt, a way of saying *you can't get rid of me even though you hate me and I hate you.* The record had forced Tibbets to keep January on one of the four second-string teams, but with the fuss they were making over the gimmick January had figured that would be far enough down the ladder to keep him out of things.

Now he wasn't so sure. Tibbets was dead. He lit another cigarette, found his hand shaking. The Camel tasted bitter. He threw it over the fence at a receding armband, and regretted it instantly. A waste. He went back inside.

Before climbing onto his bunk he got a paperback out of his footlocker. "Hey, Professor, what you reading now?" Fitch said, grinning.

January showed him the blue cover. *Winter's Tales*, by an Isak Dinesen. Fitch examined the little wartime edition. "Pretty racy, eh?"

"You bet," January said heavily. "This guy puts sex on every page." He climbed onto his bunk, opened the book. The stories were strange, hard to follow. The voices below bothered him. He concentrated harder.

As a boy on the farm in Arkansas, January had read everything he could lay his hands on. On Saturday afternoons he would race his father down the muddy lane to the mailbox (his father was a reader too), grab *The Saturday Evening Post* and run off to devour every word of it. That meant he had another week with nothing new to read, but he couldn't help it. His favorites were the Hornblower stories, but anything would do. It was a way off the farm, a way into the world. He had become a man who could slip between the covers of a book whenever he chose.

But not on this night.

THE NEXT DAY THE chaplain gave a memorial service, and on the morning after that Colonel Scholes looked in the door of their hut right after mess. "Briefing at eleven," he announced. His face was haggard. "Be there early." He looked at Fitch with bloodshot eyes, crooked a finger. "Fitch, January, Matthews—come with me."

January put on his shoes. The rest of the men sat on their bunks and watched them wordlessly. January followed Fitch and Matthews out of the hut.

"I've spent most of the night on the radio with General La May," Scholes said. He looked them each in the eye. "We've decided you're to be the first crew to make a strike."

Fitch was nodding, as if he had expected it.

"Think you can do it?" Scholes said.

"Of course," Fitch replied. Watching him January understood why they had chosen him to replace Tibbets: Fitch was like the old bull, he had that same ruthlessness. The young bull.

"Yes, sir," Matthews said.

Scholes was looking at him. "Sure," January said, not wanting to think about it. "Sure." His heart was pounding directly on his sternum. But Fitch and Matthews looked serious as owls, so he wasn't going to stick out by looking odd. It was big news, after all; anyone would be taken aback by it. Nevertheless, January made an effort to nod.

"Okay," Scholes said. "McDonald will be flying with you as copilot." Fitch frowned. "I've got to go tell those British officers that Le May doesn't want them on the strike with you. See you at the briefing."

"Yes, sir."

As soon as Scholes was around the corner Fitch swung a fist at the sky. "Yow!" Matthews cried. He and Fitch shook hands. "We did it!" Matthews took January's hand and wrung it, his face plastered with a goofy grin. "We did it!"

"Somebody did it, anyway," January said.

"Ah, Frank," Matthews said. "Show some spunk. You're always so cool."

"Old Professor Stoneface," Fitch said, glancing at January with a trace of amused contempt. "Come on, let's get to the briefing."

The briefing hut, one of the longer Quonsets, was completely surrounded by MPs holding carbines. "Gosh," Matthews said, subdued by the sight. Inside it was already smoky. The walls were covered by the usual maps of Japan. Two blackboards at the front were draped with sheets. Captain Shepard, the naval officer who worked with the scientists on the gimmick, was in back with his assistant Lieutenant Stone, winding a reel of film onto a projector. Dr. Nelson, group psychiatrist, was already seated on a front bench near the wall. Tibbets had recently sicced the psychiatrist on the group—another one of his great ideas, like the spies in the bar. The man's questions had struck January as stupid. He hadn't even been able to figure out that Easterly was a flake, something that was clear to anybody who flew with him, or even played him in a single round of poker. January slid onto a bench beside his mates.

The two Brits entered, looking furious in their stiff-upper-lip way. They sat on the bench behind January. Sweeney's and Easterly's crews filed in, followed by the other men, and soon the room was full. Fitch and the rest pulled out Lucky Strikes and lit up; since they had named the plane only January had stuck with Camels.

Scholes came in with several men January didn't recognize, and went to the front. The chatter died, and all the smoke plumes ribboned steadily into the air.

Scholes nodded, and two intelligence officers took the sheets off the blackboards, revealing aerial reconnaissance photos.

"Men," Scholes said, "these are the target cities."

Someone cleared his throat.

"In order of priority they are Hiroshima, Kokura, and Nagasaki. There will be three weather scouts: *Straight Flush* to Hiroshima, *Strange Cargo* to Kokura, and *Full House* to Nagasaki. *The Great Artiste* and *Number 91* will be accompanying the mission to take photos. And *Lucky Strike* will fly the bomb."

There were rustles, coughs. Men turned to look at January and his mates, and they all sat up straight. Sweeney stretched back to shake Fitch's hand, and there were some quick laughs. Fitch grinned.

"Now listen up," Scholes went on. "The weapon we are going to deliver was successfully tested stateside a couple of weeks ago. And now we've got orders to drop it on the enemy." He paused to let that sink in. "I'll let Captain Shepard tell you more."

Shepard walked to the blackboard slowly, savoring his entrance. His forehead was shiny with sweat, and January realized he was excited or nervous. He wondered what the psychiatrist would make of that.

"I'm going to come right to the point," Shepard said. "The bomb you are going to drop is something new in history. We think it will knock out everything within four miles."

Now the room was completely still. January noticed that he could see a great deal of his nose, eyebrows, and cheeks; it was as if he were receding back into his body, like a fox into its hole. He kept his gaze rigidly on Shepard, steadfastly ignoring the feeling. Shepard pulled a sheet back over a blackboard while someone else turned down the lights.

"This is a film of the only test we have made," Shepard said. The film started, caught, started again. A wavery cone of bright cigarette smoke speared the length of the room, and on the sheet sprang a dead gray landscape: a lot of sky, a smooth desert floor, hills in the distance. The projector went *click-click-click-click*, *click-click-click-click*. "The bomb is on top of the tower," Shepard said, and January focused on the pinlike object sticking out of the desert floor, off against the hills. It was between eight and ten miles from the camera, he judged; he had gotten good at calculating distances. He was still distracted by his face.

Click-click-click-click, click—then the screen went white for a second, filling even their room with light. When the picture returned the desert floor was filled with a white bloom of fire. The fireball coalesced and then quite suddenly it leaped off the earth all the way into the *stratosphere*, by God, like a tracer bullet leaving a machine gun, trailing a whitish pillar of smoke behind it. The pillar gushed up and a growing ball of smoke billowed outward, capping the pillar. January calculated the size of the cloud, but was sure he got it wrong. There it stood. The picture flickered, and then the screen went white again, as if the camera had melted or that part of the world had come apart. But the flapping from the projector told them it was the end of the film.

January felt the air suck in and out of his open mouth. The lights came on in the smoky room and for a second he panicked, he struggled to shove his features into an accepted pattern, the psychiatrist would be looking around at them all—and then he glanced around and realized he needn't have worried, that he wasn't alone. Faces were bloodless, eyes were blinky or bug-eyed with shock, mouths hung open or were clamped whitely shut. For a few moments they all had to acknowledge what they were doing. January, scaring himself, felt an urge to say, "Play it again, will you?" Fitch was pulling his curled black hair off his thug's forehead uneasily. Beyond him January saw that one of the Limeys had already reconsidered how mad he was about missing the flight. Now he looked sick. Someone let out a long *whew*, another whistled. January looked to the front again, where the psychiatrist watched them, undisturbed.

Shepard said, "It's big, all right. And no one knows what will happen when it's dropped from the air. But the mushroom cloud you saw will go to at least thirty thousand feet, probably sixty. And the flash you saw at the beginning was hotter than the sun."

Hotter than the sun. More licked lips, hard swallows, readjusted baseball caps. One of the intelligence officers passed out tinted goggles like welder's glasses. January took his and twiddled the opacity dial.

Scholes said, "You're the hottest thing in the armed forces, now. So no talking, even among yourselves." He took a deep breath "Let's do it the way Colonel Tibbets would have wanted us to. He picked every one of you because you were the best, and now's the time to show he was right. So—so let's make the old man proud."

The briefing was over. Men filed out into the sudden sunlight. Into the heat and glare. Captain Shepard approached Fitch. "Stone and I will be flying with you to take care of the bomb," he said.

Fitch nodded. "Do you know how many strikes we'll fly?"

"As many as it takes to make them quit." Shepard stared hard at all of them. "But it will only take one."

WAR BREEDS STRANGE DREAMS. That night January writhed over his sheets in the hot wet vegetable darkness, in that frightening half sleep when you sometimes know you are dreaming but can do nothing about it, and he dreamed he was walking …

… *walking through the streets when suddenly the sun swoops down, the sun touches down and everything is instantly darkness and smoke and silence, a deaf roaring. Walls of fire. His head hurts and in the middle of his vision is a bluewhite blur as if God's camera went off in his face. Ah—the sun fell, he thinks. His arm is burned. Blinking is painful. People stumbling by, mouths open, horribly burned—*

He is a priest, he can feel the clerical collar, and the wounded ask him for help. He points to his ears, tries to touch them but can't. Pall of black smoke over every-

thing, the city has fallen into the streets. Ah, it's the end of the world. In a park he finds shade and cleared ground. People crouch under bushes like frightened animals. Where the park meets the river red and black figures crowd into steaming water. A figure gestures from a copse of bamboo. He enters it, finds five or six faceless soldiers huddling. Their eyes have melted, their mouths are holes. Deafness spares him their words. The sighted soldier mimes drinking. The soldiers are thirsty. He nods and goes to the river in search of a container. Bodies float downstream.

Hours pass as he hunts fruitlessly for a bucket. He pulls people from the rubble. He hears a bird screeching and he realizes that his deafness is the roar of the city burning, a roar like the blood in his ears but he is not deaf, he only thought he was deaf because there are no human cries. The people are suffering in silence. Through the dusky night he stumbles back to the river, pain crashing through his head. In a field men are pulling potatoes out of the ground that have been baked well enough to eat. He shares one with them. At the river everyone is dead—

—and he struggled out of the nightmare drenched in rank sweat, the taste of dirt in his mouth, his stomach knotted with horror. He sat up and the wet rough sheet clung to his skin. His heart felt crushed between lungs desperate for air. The flowery rotting jungle smell filled him and images from the dream flashed before him so vividly that in the dim hut he saw nothing else. He grabbed his cigarettes and jumped off the bunk, hurried out into the compound. Trembling he lit up, started pacing around. For a moment he worried that the idiot psychiatrist might see him, but then he dismissed the idea. Nelson would be asleep. They were all asleep. He shook his head, looked down at his right arm and almost dropped his cigarette—but it was just his stove scar, an old scar, he'd had it most of his life, since the day he'd pulled the frypan off the stove and onto his arm, burning it with oil. He could still remember the round O of fear that his mother's mouth had made as she rushed in to see what was wrong. Just an old bum scar, he thought, let's not go overboard here. He pulled his sleeve down.

For the rest of the night he tried to walk it off, cigarette after cigarette. The dome of the sky lightened until all the compound and the jungle beyond it was visible. He was forced by the light of day to walk back into his hut and lie down as if nothing had happened.

Two DAYS LATER SCHOLES ordered them to take one of Le May's men over Rota for a test run. This new lieutenant colonel ordered Fitch not to play with the engines on takeoff. They flew a perfect run. January put the dummy gimmick right on the aiming point just as he had so often in the Salton Sea, and Fitch powered the plane down into the violent bank that started their 150-degree turn and flight for safety. Back on Tinian the lieutenant colonel congratulated them and shook each of their hands. January smiled with the rest, palms cool, heart steady. It was as if his body were a shell, something he could manipulate from without, like a bombsight. He ate well, he chatted as much as he ever had, and when the psychiatrist ran him to earth for some questions he was friendly and seemed open.

"Hello, doc."

"How do you feel about all this, Frank?"

"Just like I always have, sir. Fine."

"Eating well?"

"Better than ever."

"Sleeping well?"

"As well as I can in this humidity. I got used to

Utah, I'm afraid." Dr. Nelson laughed. Actually January had hardly slept since his dream. He was afraid of sleep. Couldn't the man see that?

"And how do you feel about being part of the crew chosen to make the first strike?"

"Well, it was the right choice, I reckon. We're the b—the best crew left."

"Do you feel sorry about Tibbets' crew's accident?"

"Yes, sir, I do." You better believe it.

After the jokes and firm handshakes that ended the interview January walked out into the blaze of the tropical noon and lit a cigarette. He allowed himself to feel how much he despised the psychiatrist and his blind profession at the same time he was waving good-bye to the man. Ounce brain. Why couldn't he have seen? Whatever happened it would be his fault .... With a rush of smoke out of him January realized how painfully easy it was to fool someone if you wanted to. All action was no more than a mask that could be perfectly manipulated from somewhere else. And all the while in that somewhere else January lived in a *click-click-click* of film, in the silent roaring of a dream, struggling against images he couldn't dispel. The heat of the tropical sun— ninety-three million miles away, wasn't it?—pulsed painfully on the back of his neck.

As he watched the psychiatrist collar their tail-gunner Kochenski, he thought of walking up to the man and saying *I quit.* I don't want to do this. In imagination he saw the look that would form in the man's eye, in Fitch's eye, in Tibbets' eye, and his mind recoiled from the idea. He felt too much contempt for them. He wouldn't for anything give them a means to despise him, a reason to call him coward. Stubbornly he banished the whole complex of thought. Easier to go along with it.

And so a couple of disjointed days later, just after midnight of August 9th, he found himself preparing for the strike. Around him Fitch and Matthews and Haddock were doing the same. How odd were the everyday motions of getting dressed when you were off to demolish a city, to end a hundred thousand lives! January found himself examining his hands, his boots, the cracks in the linoleum. He put on his survival vest, checked the pockets abstractedly for fishhooks, water kit, first aid package, emergency rations. Then the parachute harness, and his coveralls over it all. Tying his bootlaces took minutes; he couldn't do it when watching his fingers so closely.

"Come on, Professor!" Fitch's voice was tight. "The big day is here."

He followed the others into the night. A cool wind was blowing. The chaplain said a prayer for them. They took jeeps down Broadway to runway Able. *Lucky Strike* stood in a circle of spotlights and men, half of them with cameras, the rest with reporter's pads. They surrounded the crew; it reminded January of a Hollywood premiere. Eventually he escaped up the hatch and into the plane. Others followed. Half an hour passed before Fitch joined them, grinning like a movie star. They started the engines, and January was thankful for their vibrating, thought-smothering roar. They taxied away from the Hollywood scene and January felt relief for a moment until he remembered where they were going. On runway Able the engines pitched up to their twenty-three hundred rpm whine, and looking out the clear windscreen he saw the runway paint-marks move by ever faster. Fitch kept them on the runway till Tinian had run out from under them, then quickly pulled up.

They were on their way.

WHEN THEY GOT TO altitude January climbed past Fitch and McDonald to the bombardier's seat and placed his parachute on it. He leaned back. The roar of the four engines packed around him like cotton batting. He was on the flight, nothing to be done about it now. The heavy vibration was a comfort, he liked the feel of it there in the nose of the plane. A drowsy, sad acceptance hummed through him.

Against his closed eyelids flashed a black eyeless face and he jerked awake, heart racing. He was on the flight, no way out. Now he realized how easy it would have been to get out of it. He could have just said he didn't want to. The simplicity of it appalled him. Who gave a damn what the psychiatrist or Tibbets or anyone else thought, compared to this? Now there was no way out. It was a comfort, in a way. Now he could stop worrying, stop thinking he had any choice.

Sitting there with his knees bracketing the bombsight January dozed, and as he dozed he daydreamed his way out. He could climb the step to Fitch and McDonald and declare he had been secretly promoted to major and ordered to redirect the mission. They were to go to Tokyo and drop the bomb in the bay. The Jap War Cabinet had been told to watch this demonstration of the new weapon, and when they saw that fireball boil the bay and bounce into heaven they'd run and sign surrender papers as fast as they could write, kamikazes or not. They weren't crazy, after all. No need to murder a whole city. It was such a good plan that the generals back home were no doubt changing the mission at this very minute, desperately radioing their instructions to Tinian, only to find out it was too late ... so that when they returned to Tinian January would become a hero for guessing what the generals really wanted, and for risking all to do it. It would be like one of the Horn-blower stories in *The Saturday Evening Post*.

Once again January jerked awake. The drowsy pleasure of the fantasy was replaced with desperate scorn. There wasn't a chance in hell that he could convince Fitch and the rest that he had secret orders superseding theirs. And he couldn't go up there and wave his pistol around and *order* them to drop the bomb in Tokyo Bay, because he was the one who had to actually drop it, and he couldn't be down in front dropping the bomb and up ordering the others around at the same time. Pipe dreams.

Time swept on, slow as a second hand. January's thoughts, however, matched the spin of the props; desperately they cast about, now this way now that, like an animal caught by the leg in a trap. The crew was silent. The clouds below were a white scree on the black ocean. January's knee vibrated against the squat stand of the bombsight. He was the one who had to drop the bomb. No matter where his thoughts lunged they were brought up short by that. He was the one, not Fitch or the crew, not Le May, not the generals and scientists back home, not Truman and his advisors. Truman—suddenly January hated him. Roosevelt would have done it differently. If only Roosevelt had lived! The grief that had filled January when he learned of Roosevelt's death reverberated through him again, more strongly than ever. It was unfair to have worked so hard and then not see the war's end. And FDR would have ended it differently. Back at the start of it all he had declared that civilian centers were never to be bombed, and if he had lived, if, if, if. But he hadn't. And now it was smiling bastard Harry Truman, ordering *him*, Frank January, to drop the sun on two hundred thousand women and children. Once his father had taken him to see the Browns play before twenty thousand, a giant crowd— "I never voted for you," January whispered viciously, and jerked to realize he had spoken aloud. Luckily his microphone was off. But Roosevelt would have done it differently, he *would have*.

The bombsight rose before him, spearing the black sky and blocking some of the hundreds of little cruciform stars. *Lucky Strike* ground on toward Iwo Jima, minute by minute flying four miles closer to their target. January leaned forward and put his face in the cool headrest of the bombsight, hoping that its grasp might hold his thoughts as well as his forehead. It worked surprisingly well.

His earphones crackled and he sat up. "Captain January," It was Shepard. "We're going to arm the bomb now, want to watch?"

"Sure thing." He shook his head, surprised at his own duplicity. Stepping up between the pilots, he moved stiffly to the roomy cabin behind the cockpit. Matthews was at his desk taking a navigational fix on the radio signals from Iwo Jima and Okinawa, and Haddock stood beside him. At the back of the compartment was a small circular hatch, below the larger tunnel leading to the rear of the plane. January opened it, sat down and swung himself feet first through the hole.

The bomb bay was unheated, and the cold air felt good. He stood facing the bomb. Stone was sitting on the floor of the bay; Shepard was laid out under the bomb, reaching into it. On a rubber pad next to Stone were tools, plates, several cylindrical blocks. Shepard pulled back, sat up, sucked a scraped knuckle. He shook his head ruefully: "I don't dare wear gloves with this one."

"I'd be just as happy myself if you didn't let something slip," January joked nervously. The two men laughed.

"Nothing can blow till I change those green wires to the red ones," Stone said.

"Give me the wrench," Shepard said. Stone handed it to him, and he stretched under the bomb again. After some awkward wrenching inside it he lifted out a cylindrical plug. "Breech plug," he said, and set it on the mat.

January found his skin goose-pimpling in the cold air. Stone handed Shepard one of the blocks. Shepard extended under the bomb again. "Red ends toward the breech." "I know." Watching them January was reminded of auto mechanics on the oily floor of a garage, working under a car. He had spent a few years doing that himself, after his family moved to Vicksburg. Hiroshima was a river town. One time a flatbed truck carrying bags of cement powder down Fourth Street hill had lost its brakes and careened into the intersection with River Road, where despite the driver's efforts to turn it smashed into a passing car. Frank had been out in the yard playing, had heard the crash and saw the cement dust rising. He had been one of the first there. The woman and child in the passenger seat of the Model T had been killed. The woman driving was okay. They were from Chicago. A group of folks subdued the driver of the truck, who kept trying to help at the Model T, though he had a bad cut on his head and was covered with white dust.

"Okay, let's tighten the breech plug." Stone gave Shepard the wrench. "Sixteen turns exactly," Shepard said. He was sweating even in the bay's chill, and he paused to wipe his forehead. "Let's hope we don't get hit by lightning." He put the wrench down and shifted onto his knees, picked up a circular plate. Hubcap, January thought. Stone connected wires, then helped Shepard install two more plates. Good old American know-how, January thought, goose pimples rippling across his skin like cat's paws over water. There was Shepard, a scientist, putting together a bomb like he was an auto mechanic changing oil and plugs. January felt a tight rush of rage at the scientists who had designed the bomb. They had worked on it for over a year down there in New Mexico, had none of them in all that time ever stopped to think what they were doing?

But none of them had to drop it. January turned to hide his face from Shepard, stepped down the bay. The bomb looked like a big long trash can, with fins at one end and little antennae at the other. Just a bomb, he thought, damn it, it's just another bomb.

Shepard stood and patted the bomb gently. "We've got a live one now." Never a thought about what it would do. January hurried by the man, afraid that hatred would crack his shell and give him away. The pistol strapped to his belt caught on the hatchway and he imagined shooting Shepard—shooting Fitch and McDonald and plunging the controls forward so that *Lucky Strike* tilted and spun down into the sea like a spent tracer bullet, like a plane broken by flak, following the arc of all human ambition. Nobody would ever know what had happened to them, and their trash can would be dumped at the bottom of the Pacific where it belonged. He could even shoot everyone and parachute out, and perhaps be rescued by one of the Superdumbos following them....

The thought passed and remembering it January squinted with disgust. But another part of him agreed that it was a possibility. It could be done. It would solve his problem. His fingers explored his holster snap.

"Want some coffee?" Matthews asked.

"Sure," January said, and took his hand from the gun to reach for the cup. He sipped: hot. He watched Matthews and Benton tune the loran equipment. As the beeps came in Matthews took a straightedge and drew lines from Okinawa and Iwo Jima on his map table. He tapped a finger on the intersection. "They've taken the art out of navigation," he said to January. "They might as well stop making the navigator's dome," thumbing up at the little Plexiglas bubble over them.

"Good old American know-how," January said.

Matthews nodded. With two fingers he measured the distance between their position and Iwo Jima. Benton measured with a ruler.

"Rendezvous at five thirty-five, eh?" Matthews said. They were to rendezvous with the two trailing planes over Iwo.

Benton disagreed: "I'd say five-fifty."

"What? Check again, guy, we're not in no tugboat here."

"The wind—"

"Yah, the wind. Frank, you want to add a bet to the pool?"

"Five thirty-six," January said promptly.

They laughed. "See, he's got more confidence in me," Matthews said with a dopey grin.

January recalled his plan to shoot the crew and tip the plane into the sea, and he pursed his lips, repelled. Not for anything would he be able to shoot these men, who, if not friends, were at least companions. They passed for friends. They meant no harm.

Shepard and Stone climbed into the cabin. Matthews offered them coffee. "The gimmick's ready to kick their ass, eh?" Shepard nodded and drank.

January moved forward, past Haddock's console. Another plan that wouldn't work. What to do? All the flight engineer's dials and gauges showed conditions were normal. Maybe he could sabotage something? Cut a line somewhere?

Fitch looked back at him and said, "When are we due over Iwo?"

"Five-forty, Matthews says."

"He better be right."

A thug. In peacetime Fitch would be hanging around a pool table giving the cops trouble. He was perfect for war. Tibbets had chosen his men well—most of them, anyway. Moving back past Haddock, January stopped to stare at the group of men in the navigation cabin. They joked, drank coffee. They were all a bit like Fitch: young toughs, capable and thoughtless. They were having a good time, an adventure. That was January's dominant impression of his companions in the 509th; despite all the bitching and the occasional moments of overmastering fear, they were having a good time. His mind spun forward and he saw what these young men would grow up to be like as clearly as if they stood before him in businessmen's suits, prosperous and balding. They would be tough and capable and thoughtless, and as the years passed and the great war receded in time they would look back on it with ever-increasing nostalgia, for they would be the survivors and not the dead. Every year of this war would feel like ten in their memories, so that the war would always remain the central experience of their lives—a time when history lay palpable in their hands, when each of their daily acts affected it, when moral issues were simple, and others told them what to do—so that as more years passed and the survivors aged, bodies falling apart, lives in one rut or another, they would unconsciously push harder and harder to thrust the world into war again, thinking somewhere inside themselves that if they could only return to world war then they would magically be again as they were in the last one—young, and free, and happy. And by that time they would hold the positions of power, they would be capable of doing it.

So there would be more wars, January saw. He heard it in Matthews' laughter, saw it in their excited eyes. "There's Iwo and it's five thirty-one. Pay up! I win!" And in future wars they'd have more bombs like the gimmick, hundreds of them no doubt. He saw more planes, more young crews like this one, flying to Moscow no doubt or to wherever, fireballs in every capital, why not? And to what end? To what end? So that the old men could hope to become magically young again. Nothing more sane than that.

They were over Iwo Jima. Three more hours to Japan. Voices from *The Great Artiste* and *Number 91* crackled on radio. Rendezvous accomplished, the three planes flew northwest, toward Shikoku, the first Japanese island in their path. January went aft to use the toilet. "You okay, Frank?" Matthews asked. "Sure. Terrible coffee, though." "Ain't it always." January tugged at his baseball cap and hurried away. Kochenski and the other gunners were playing poker. When he was done he returned forward. Matthews sat on the stool before his maps, readying his equipment for the constant monitoring of drift that would now be required. Haddock and Benton were also busy at their stations. January maneuvered between the pilots down into the nose. "Good shooting," Matthews called after him.

Forward it seemed quieter. January got settled, put his headphones on and leaned forward to look out the ribbed Plexiglas.

Dawn had turned the whole vault of the sky pink. Slowly the radiant shade shifted through lavender to blue, pulse by pulse a different color. The ocean below was a glittering blue plane, marbled by a pattern of puffy pink cloud. The sky above was a vast dome, darker above than on the horizon. January had always thought that dawn was the time when you could see most clearly how big the earth was, and how high above it they flew. It seemed they flew at the very upper edge of the atmosphere, and January saw how thin it was, how it was just a skin of air really, so that even if you flew up to its top the earth still extended away infinitely in every direction. The coffee had warmed January, he was sweating. Sunlight blinked off the Plexiglas. His watch said six. Plane and hemisphere of blue were split down the middle by the bombsight. His earphones crackled and he listened in to the reports from the lead planes flying over the target cities. Kokura, Nagasaki, Hiroshima, all of them had six-tenths cloud cover. Maybe they would have to cancel the whole mission because of weather. "We'll look at Hiroshima first," Fitch said. January peered down at the fields of miniature clouds with renewed interest. His parachute slipped under him. Readjusting it he imagined putting it on, sneaking back to the central escape hatch under the navigator's cabin, opening the hatch . . . he could be out of the plane and gone before anyone noticed. Leave it up to them. They could bomb or not but it wouldn't be January's doing. He could float down onto the world like a puff of dandelion, feel cool air rush around him, watch the silk canopy dome hang over him like a miniature sky, a private world.

An eyeless black face. January shuddered; it was

as though the nightmare could return any time. If he jumped nothing would change, the bomb would still fall—would he feel any better, floating on his Inland Sea? Sure, one part of him shouted; maybe, another conceded; the rest of him saw that face….

Earphones crackled. Shepard said, "Lieutenant Stone has now armed the bomb, and I can tell you all what we are carrying. Aboard with us is the world's first atomic bomb."

Not exactly, January thought. Whistles squeaked in his earphones. The first one went off in New Mexico. Splitting atoms: January had heard the term before. Tremendous energy in every atom, Einstein had said. Break one, and—he had seen the result on film. Shepard was talking about radiation, which brought back more to January. Energy released in the form of X rays. Killed by X rays! It would be against the Geneva Convention if they had thought of it.

Fitch cut in. "When the bomb is dropped Lieutenant Benton will record our reaction to what we see. This recording is being made for history, so watch your language." Watch your language! January choked back a laugh. Don't curse or blaspheme God at the sight of the first atomic bomb incinerating city and all its inhabitants with X rays!

Six-twenty. January found his hands clenched together on the headrest of the bombsight. He felt as if he had a fever. In the harsh wash of morning light the skin on the backs of his hands appeared slightly translucent. The whorls in the skin looked like the delicate patterning of waves on the sea's surface. His hands were made of atoms. Atoms were the smallest building block of matter, it took billions of them to make those tense, trembling hands. Split one atom and you had the fireball. That

meant that the energy contained in even one hand …
he turned up a palm to look at the lines and the mottled
flesh under the transparent skin. A person was a bomb
that could blow up the world. January felt that latent
power stir in him, pulsing with every hard heart-knock.
What beings they were, and in what a blue expanse of a
world! –And here they spun on to drop a bomb and kill
a hundred thousand of these astonishing beings.

When a fox or raccoon is caught by the leg in a
trap, it lunges until the leg is frayed, twisted, perhaps
broken, and only then does the animal's pain and exhaustion force it to quit. Now in the same way January
wanted to quit. His mind hurt. His plans to escape were
so much crap—stupid, useless. Better to quit. He tried
to stop thinking, but it was hopeless. How could he
stop? As long as he was conscious he would be thinking.
The mind struggles longer in its traps than any fox.

Lucky Strike tilted up and began the long climb to
bombing altitude. On the horizon the clouds lay over
a green island. Japan. Surely it had gotten hotter, the
heater must be broken, he thought. Don't think. Every
few minutes Matthews gave Fitch small course adjustments. "Two seventy-five, now. That's it." To escape
the moment January recalled his childhood. Following
a mule and plow. Moving to Vicksburg (rivers). For a
while there in Vicksburg, since his stutter made it hard
to gain friends, he had played a game with himself. He
had passed the time by imagining that everything he
did was vitally important and determined the fate of
the world. If he crossed a road in front of a certain car,
for instance, then the car wouldn't make it through the
next intersection before a truck hit it, and so the man
driving would be killed and wouldn't be able to invent
the flying boat that would save President Wilson from

kidnappers—so he had to wait for that car because everything afterward depended on it. Oh damn it, he thought, damn it, think of something *different*. The last Hornblower story he had read—how would *he* get out of this? The round 0 of his mother's face as she ran in and saw his arm—The Mississippi, mud-brown behind its levees—Abruptly he shook his head, face twisted in frustration and despair, aware at last that no possible avenue of memory would serve as an escape for him now, for now there was no part of his life that did not apply to the situation he was in, and no matter where he cast his mind it was going to shore up against the hour facing him.

Less than an hour. They were at thirty thousand feet, bombing altitude. Fitch gave him altimeter readings to dial into the bombsight. Matthews gave him wind-speeds. Sweat got in his eye and he blinked furiously. The sun rose behind them like an atomic bomb, glinting off every corner and edge of the Plexiglas, illuminating his bubble compartment with a fierce glare. Broken plans jumbled together in his mind, his breath was short, his throat dry. Uselessly and repeatedly he damned the scientists, damned Truman. Damned the Japanese causing the whole mess in the first place, damned yellow killers, they had brought this on themselves. Remember Pearl. American men had died under bombs when no war had been declared; they had started it and now it was coming back to them with a vengeance. And they deserved it. And an invasion of Japan would take years, cost millions of lives—end it now, end it, they deserved it, they deserved it steaming river full of charcoal people silently dying damned stubborn race of maniacs!

"There's Honshu," Fitch said, and January returned to the plane. They were over the Inland Sea. Soon they would pass the secondary target, Kokura, a bit to the south. Seven-thirty. The island was draped more heavily than the sea by clouds, and again January's heart leaped with the idea that weather would cancel the mission. But they did deserve it. It was a mission like any other mission. He had dropped bombs on Africa, Sicily, Italy, all Germany.... He leaned forward to take a look through the sight. Under the X of the crosshairs was the sea, but at the lead edge of the sight was land. Honshu. At two hundred and thirty miles an hour that gave them about a half hour to Hiroshima. Maybe less. He wondered if his heart could beat so hard for that long.

Fitch said, "Matthews, I'm giving over guidance to you. Just tell us what to do."

"Bear south two degrees," was all Matthews said. At last their voices had taken on a touch of awareness, even fear.

"January, are you ready?" Fitch asked.

"I'm just waiting," January said. He sat up, so Fitch could see the back of his head. The bombsight stood between his legs. A switch on its side would start the bombing sequence; the bomb would not leave the plane immediately upon the flick of the switch, but would drop after a fifteen second radio tone warned the following planes. The sight was adjusted accordingly.

"Adjust to a heading of two sixty-five," Matthews said. "We're coming in directly upwind." This was to make any side-drift adjustments for the bomb unnecessary. "January, dial it down to two hundred and thirty-one miles per hour."

"Two thirty-one."

Fitch said, "Everyone but January and Matthews, get your goggles on."

January took the darkened goggles from the

floor. One needed to protect one's eyes or they might melt. He put them on, put his forehead on the head-rest. They were in the way. He took them off. When he looked through the sight again there was land under the crosshairs. He checked his watch. Eight o'clock. Up and reading the papers, drinking tea.

"Ten minutes to AP," Matthews said. The aiming point was Aioi Bridge, a T-shaped bridge in the middle of the delta-straddling city. Easy to recognize.

"There's a lot of cloud down there," Fitch nodded. "Are you going to be able to see?"

"I won't be sure until we try it," January said.

"We can make another pass and use radar if we need to," Matthews said.

Fitch said. "Don't drop it unless you're sure, January."

"Yes, sir."

Through the sight a grouping of rooftops and gray roads was just visible between broken clouds. Around it green forest. "All right," Matthews exclaimed, "here we go! Keep it right on this heading, Captain! January, we'll stay at two thirty-one."

"And same heading," Fitch said. "January, she's all yours. Everyone make sure your goggles are on. And be ready for the turn."

January's world contracted to the view through the bombsight. A stippled field of cloud and forest. Over a small range of hills and into Hiroshima's watershed. The broad river was mud brown, the land pale hazy green, the growing network of roads flat gray. Now the tiny rectangular shapes of buildings covered almost all the land, and swimming into the sight the city proper, narrow islands thrusting into a dark blue bay. Under the crosshairs the city moved island by island, cloud by cloud. January had stopped breathing, his fingers were rigid as stone on the switch. And there was Aioi Bridge. It slid right under the crosshairs, a tiny T right in a gap in the clouds. January's fingers crushed the switch. Deliberately he took a breath, held it. Clouds swam under the crosshairs, then the next island. Almost there he said calmly into his microphone, "Steady." Now that he was committed his heart was humming like the Wrights. He counted to ten. Now flowing under the crosshairs were clouds alternating with green forest, leaden roads. "I've turned the switch, but I'm not getting a tone!" he croaked into the mike. His right hand held the switch firmly in place. Fitch shouting something—Matthews' voice cracked across it—"Flipping it b-back and forth," January shouted, shielding the bombsight with his body from the eyes of the pilots. "But still—wait a second—"

He pushed the switch down. A low hum filled his ears. "That's it! It started!"

"But where will it land?" Matthews cried.

"Hold steady!" January shouted.

Lucky Strike shuddered and lofted up ten or twenty feet. January twisted to look down and there was the bomb, flying just below the plane. Then with a wobble it fell away.

The plane banked right and dove so hard that the centrifugal threw January against the Plexiglas. Several thousand feet lower Fitch leveled it out and they hurtled north.

"Do you see anything?" Fitch cried.

From the tail gun Kochenski gasped "Nothing." January struggled upright. He reached for the welder's goggles, but they were no longer on his head. He couldn't find them. "How long has it been?" he said.

"Thirty seconds," Matthews replied.

January clamped his eyes shut.

The blood in his eyelids lit up red, then white.

On the earphones a clutter of voices: "Oh my God. Oh my God." The plane bounced and tumbled, metallically shrieking. January pressed himself off the Plexiglas. "Nother shockwave!" Kochenski yelled. The plane rocked again, bounced out of control, this is it, January thought, end of the world, I guess that solves my problem.

He opened his eyes and found he could still see. The engines still roared, the props spun. "Those were the shockwaves from the bomb," Fitch called. "We're okay now. Look at that! Will you look at that sonofabitch go!"

January looked. The cloud layer below had burst apart, and a black column of smoke billowed up from a core of red fire. Already the top of the column was at their height. Exclamations of shock clattered painfully in January's ears. He stared at the fiery base of the cloud, at the scores of fires feeding into it. Suddenly he could see past the cloud, and his fingernails cut into his palms. Through a gap in the clouds he saw it clearly, the delta, the six rivers, there off to the left of the tower of smoke: the city of Hiroshima, untouched.

"We missed!" Kochenski yelled. "We missed it!"

January turned to hide his face from the pilots; on it was a grin like a rictus. He sat back in his seat and let the relief fill him.

Then it was back to it. "God damn it!" Fitch shouted down at him. McDonald was trying to restrain him. "January, get up here!"

"Yes, sir." Now there was a new set of problems.

January stood and turned, legs weak. His right fingertips throbbed painfully. The men were crowded forward to look out the Plexiglas. January looked with them.

The mushroom cloud was forming. It roiled out as if it might continue to extend forever, fed by the inferno and the black stalk below it. It looked about two miles wide, and a half mile tall, and it extended well above the height they flew at, dwarfing their plane entirely. "Do you think we'll all be sterile?" Matthews said.

"I can taste the radiation," McDonald declared. "Can you? It tastes like lead."

Bursts of flame shot up into the cloud from below, giving a purplish tint to the stalk. There it stood: lifelike, malignant, sixty thousand feet tall. One bomb. January shoved past the pilots into the navigation cabin, overwhelmed.

"Should I start recording everyone's reactions, Captain?" asked Benton.

"To hell with that," Fitch said, following January back. Shepard got there first, descending quickly from the navigation dome. He rushed across the cabin, caught January on the shoulder, "You bastard!" he screamed as January stumbled back. "You lost your nerve, coward!"

January went for Shepard, happy to have a target at last, but Fitch cut in and grabbed him by the collar, pulled him around until they were face to face—

"Is that right?" Fitch cried, as angry as Shepard. "Did you screw up on purpose?"

"No," January grunted, and knocked Fitch's hands away from his neck. He swung and smacked Fitch on the mouth, caught him solid. Fitch staggered back, recovered, and no doubt would have beaten January up, but Matthews and Benton and Stone leaped in and held him back, shouting for order. "Shut up! Shut up!" McDonald screamed from the cockpit, and for a moment it was bedlam, but Fitch let himself be restrained, and soon only McDonald's shouts for quiet were heard. January retreated to between the pilot seats, right hand on his pistol holster.

The city was in the crosshairs when I flipped the switch," he said. 'But the first couple of times I flipped it nothing happened—"

"That's a lie!" Shepard shouted. "There was nothing wrong with the switch, I checked it myself. Besides, the bomb exploded *miles* beyond Hiroshima, look for yourself! That's *minutes*." He wiped spit from his chin and pointed at January. "You did it."

"You don't know that," January said. But he could see the men had been convinced by Shepard, and he took a step back. "You just get me to a board of inquiry, quick. And leave me alone till then. If you touch me again," glaring venomously at Fitch and then Shepard, "I'll shoot you." He turned and hopped down to his seat, feeling exposed and vulnerable, like a treed raccoon.

"They'll shoot *you* for this," Shepard screamed after him. "Disobeying orders—treason—" Matthews and Stone were shutting him up.

"Let's get out of here," he heard McDonald say. "I can taste the lead, can't you?"

January looked out the Plexiglas. The giant cloud still burned and roiled. One atom … Well, they had really done it to that forest. He almost laughed but stopped himself, afraid of hysteria. Through a break in the clouds he got a clear view of Hiroshima for the first time. It laid spread over its islands like a map, unharmed. Well, that was that. The inferno at the base of the mushroom cloud was eight or ten miles around the shore of the bay and a mile or two inland. A certain patch of forest would be gone, destroyed—utterly blasted from the face of the earth. The Japs would be able to go out and investigate the damage. And if they were told it was a demonstration, a warning—and if they acted fast—well, they had their chance. Maybe it would work.

The release of tension made January feel sick. Then he recalled Shepard's words and he knew that whether his plan worked or not he was still in trouble. In trouble! It was worse than that. Bitterly he cursed the Japanese, he even wished for a moment that he *had* dropped it on them. Wearily he let his despair empty him.

A long while later he sat up straight. Once again he was a trapped animal. He began lunging for escape, casting about for plans. One alternative after another. All during the long grim flight home he considered it, mind spinning at the speed of the props and beyond. And when they came down on Tinian he had a plan. It was a long shot, he reckoned, but it was the best he could do.

The briefing hut was surrounded by MPs again. January stumbled back from the truck with the rest and walked inside. He was more than ever aware of the looks given him, and they were hard, accusatory. He was too tired to care. He hadn't slept more than thirty-six hours, and had slept very little since last time he had been in the hut, a week before. Now the room quivered with the lack of engine vibration to stabilize it, and the silence roared. It was all he could do to hold on to the bare essentials of his plan. The glares of Fitch and Shepard, the hurt incomprehension of Matthews, they had to be thrust out of his focus. Thankfully he lit a cigarette.

In a clamor of question and argument the others described the strike. Then the haggard Scholes and an intelligence officer led them through the bombing run. January's plan made it necessary to hold to his story: ". . . and when the AP got under the crosshairs I pushed down the switch, but got no signal. I flipped it up and down repeatedly until the tone kicked in. At that point there was still fifteen seconds to release."

"Was there anything that may have caused the tone to start when it did?"

"Not that I noticed immediately, but—"

"It's impossible," Shepard interrupted, face red. "I checked the switch before we flew and there was nothing wrong with it. Besides, the drop occurred over a minute—"

"Captain Shepard," Scholes said. "We'll hear from you presently."

"But he's obviously lying—"

"Captain Shepard! It's not at all obvious. Don't speak unless questioned."

"Anyway," January said, hoping to shift the questions away from the issue of the long delay, "I noticed something about the bomb when it was falling that could explain why it stuck. I need to discuss it with one of the scientists familiar with the bomb's design."

"What was that?" Scholes asked suspiciously.

January hesitated. "There's going to be an inquiry, right?"

Scholes frowned. "This is the inquiry, Captain January. Tell us what you saw."

"But there will be some proceeding beyond this one?"

"It looks like there's going to be a court-martial, yes, Captain."

"That's what I thought. I don't want to talk to anyone but my counsel, and some scientist familiar with the bomb."

"*I'm* a scientist familiar with the bomb," Shepard burst out. "You could tell me if you really had anything, you—"

"I said I need a scientist!" January exclaimed, rising to face the scarlet Shepard across the table. "Not a G-God damned mechanic." Shepard started to shout, others joined in and the room rang with argument. While Scholes restored order January sat down, and he refused to be drawn out again.

"I'll see you're assigned counsel, and initiate the court martial," Scholes said, clearly at a loss. "Meanwhile you are under arrest, on suspicion of disobeying orders in combat." January nodded, and Scholes gave him over to the MPs.

"One last thing," January said, fighting exhaustion. "Tell General Le May that if the Japs are told this drop was a warning, it might have the same effect as—"

"I told you!" Shepard shouted. "I told you he did it on purpose!"

Men around Shepard restrained him. But he had convinced most of them, and even Matthews stared at him with surprised anger.

January shook his head wearily. He had the dull feeling that his plan, while it had succeeded so far, was ultimately not a good one. "Just trying to make the best of it." It took all of his remaining will to force his legs to carry him in a dignified manner out of the hut.

HIS CELL WAS AN empty NCO's office. MPs brought his meals. For the first couple of days he did little but sleep. On the third day he glanced out the office's barred window, and saw a tractor pulling a tarpaulin-draped trolley out of the compound, followed by jeeps filled with MPs. It looked like a military funeral. January rushed to the door and banged on it until one of the young MPs came.

"What's that they're doing out there?" January demanded.

Eyes cold and mouth twisted, the MP said, "They're making another strike. They're going to do it right this time."

"No!" January cried. "No!" He rushed the MP, who knocked him back and locked the door. "*No!*" He beat the door until his hands hurt, cursing wildly. "You don't *need* to do it. It isn't *necessary*." Shell shattered at last, he collapsed on the bed and wept. Now everything he had done would be rendered meaningless. He had sacrificed himself for nothing.

A DAY OR TWO after that the MPs led in a colonel, an iron-haired man who stood stiffly and crushed January's hand when he shook it. His eyes were a pale, icy blue.

"I am Colonel Dray," he said. "I have been ordered to defend you in court-martial." January could feel the dislike pouring from the man. "To do that I'm going to need every fact you have, so let's get started."

"I'm not talking to anybody until I've seen an atomic scientist."

"I am your *defense* counsel—"

"I don't care who you are," January said. "Your defense of me depends on you getting one of the scientists *here*. The higher up he is, the better. And I want to speak to him alone."

"I will have to be present."

So he would do it. But now January's lawyer, too, was an enemy.

"Naturally," January said. "You're my lawyer. But no one else. Our atomic secrecy may depend on it."

"You saw evidence of sabotage?"

"Not one word more until that scientist is here."

Angrily the colonel nodded and left.

LATE THE NEXT DAY the colonel returned with another man. "This is Dr. Forest."

"I helped develop the bomb," Forest said. He had a crew cut and dressed in fatigues, and to January he looked more Army than the colonel. Suspiciously he stared back and forth at the two men.

"You'll vouch for this man's identity on your word as an officer?" he asked Dray.

"Of course," the colonel said stiffly, offended.

"So," Dr. Forest said. "You had some trouble getting it off when you wanted to. Tell me what you saw."

"I saw nothing," January said harshly. He took a deep breath; it was time to commit himself. "I want you to take a message back to the scientists. You folks have been working on this thing for years, and you must have had time to consider how the bomb should have been used. You know we could have convinced the Japs to surrender by showing them a demonstration—"

"Wait a minute," Forest said. "You're saying you didn't see anything? There wasn't a malfunction?"

"That's right," January said, and cleared his throat. "It wasn't *necessary*, do you understand?"

Forest was looking at Colonel Dray. Dray gave him a disgusted shrug. "He told me he saw evidence of sabotage."

"I want you to go back and ask the scientists to intercede for me," January said, raising his voice to get the man's attention. "I haven't got a chance in that court-martial. But if the scientists defend me then maybe they'll let me live, see? I don't want to get shot for doing something every one of you scientists would have done."

Dr. Forest had backed away. Color rising, he said, "What makes you think that's what we would have done? Don't you think we considered it? Don't you think men better qualified than you made the decision?" He waved a hand— "God damn it—what made you think you were competent to decide something as important as that!"

January was appalled at the man's reaction; in his plan it had gone differently. Angrily he jabbed a finger at Forest. "Because *I* was the man doing it, *Doctor* Forest. You take even one step back from that and suddenly you can pretend it's not your doing. Fine for you, but *I was there*."

At every word the man's color was rising. It looked like he might pop a vein in his neck. January tried once more. "Have you ever tried to imagine what one of your bombs would do to a city full of people?"

"I've had enough!" the man exploded. He turned to Dray. "I'm under no obligation to keep what I've heard here confidential. You can be sure it will be used as evidence in Captain January's court-martial." He turned and gave January a look of such blazing hatred that January understood it. For these men to admit he was right would mean admitting that they were wrong—that every one of them was responsible for his part in the construction of the weapon January had refused to use. Understanding that, January knew he was doomed.

The bang of Dr. Forest's departure still shook the little office. January sat on his cot, got out a smoke. Under Colonel Dray's cold gaze he lit one shakily, took a drag. He looked up at the colonel, shrugged. "It was my best chance," he explained. That did something—for the first and only time the cold disdain in the colonel's eyes shifted to a little, hard, lawyerly gleam of respect.

THE COURT-MARTIAL LASTED two days. The verdict was guilty of disobeying orders in combat and of giving aid and comfort to the enemy. The sentence was death by firing squad.

FOR MOST OF HIS remaining days January rarely spoke, drawing ever further behind the mask that had hidden him for so long. A clergyman came to see him, but it was the 509th's chaplain, the one who had said the prayer blessing the *Lucky Strike's* mission before they took off. Angrily January sent him packing.

Later, however, a young Catholic priest dropped by. His name was Patrick Getty. He was a little pudgy man, bespectacled and, it seemed, somewhat afraid of January. January let the man talk to him. When he returned the next day January talked back a bit, and on the day after that he talked some more. It became a habit.

Usually January talked about his childhood. He talked of plowing mucky black bottom land behind a mule. Of running down the lane to the mailbox. Of reading books by the light of the moon after he had been ordered to sleep, and of being beaten by his mother for it with a high-heeled shoe. He told the priest the story of the time his arm had been burnt, and about the car crash at the bottom of Fourth Street. "It's the truck driver's face I remember, do you see, Father?"

"Yes," the young priest said. "Yes."

And he told him about the game he had played in which every action he took tipped the balance of world affairs. "When I remembered that game I thought it was dumb. Step on a sidewalk crack and cause an earthquake—you know, it's stupid. Kids are like that." The priest nodded. "But now I've been thinking that if everybody were to live their whole like that, thinking that every move they made really was important, then ... it might make a difference." He waved a hand vaguely, expelled cigarette smoke. "You're accountable for what you do."

"Yes," the priest said. "Yes, you are."

"And if you're given orders to do something wrong, you're still accountable, right? The orders don't change it."

"That's right."

"Hmph." January smoked a while. "So they say, anyway. But look what happens." He waved at the office. "I'm like the guy in a story I read—he thought everything in books was true, and after reading a bunch of westerns he tried to rob a train. They tossed him in jail." He laughed shortly. "Books are full of crap."

"Not all of them," the priest said. "Besides, you weren't trying to rob a train."

They laughed at the notion. "Did you read that story?"

"No."

"It was the strangest book—there were two stories in it, and they alternated chapter by chapter, but they didn't have a thing to do with each other! I didn't get it."

" ... Maybe the writer was trying to say that everything connects to everything else."

"Maybe. But it's a funny way to say it."

"I like it."

And so they passed the time, talking.

o o o

So IT WAS THE priest who was the one to come by

and tell January that his request for a Presidential pardon had been refused. Getty said awkwardly, "It seems the President approves the sentence."

"That bastard," January said weakly. He sat on his cot.

Time passed. It was another hot, humid day.

"Well," the priest said. "Let me give you some better news. Given your situation I don't think telling you matters, though I've been told not to. The second mission—you know there was a second strike?"

"Yes."

"Well, they missed too."

"What?" January cried, and bounced to his feet. "You're kidding!"

"No. They flew to Kokura, but found it covered by clouds. It was the same over Nagasaki and Hiroshima, so they flew back to Kokura and tried to drop the bomb using radar to guide it, but apparently there was a—a genuine equipment failure this time, and the bomb fell on an island."

January was hopping up and down, mouth hanging open, "So we n-never—"

"We never dropped an atom bomb on a Japanese city. That's right." Getty grinned. "And get this—I heard this from my superior—they sent a message to the Japanese government telling them that the two explosions were warnings, and that if they didn't surrender by September first we would drop bombs on Kyoto and Tokyo, and then wherever else we had to. Word is that the Emperor went to Hiroshima to survey the damage; and when he saw it he ordered the Cabinet to surrender. So …"

"So it worked," January said. He hopped around, "It worked, it worked!"

"Yes."

"Just like I said it would!" he cried, and hopping before the priest he laughed.

Getty was jumping around a little too, and the sight of the priest bouncing was too much for January. He sat on his cot and laughed till the tears ran down his cheeks.

"So—" he sobered quickly. "So Truman's going to shoot me anyway, eh?"

"Yes," the priest said unhappily. "I guess that's right."

This time January's laugh was bitter. "He's a bastard, all right. And proud of being a bastard, which makes it worse." He shook his head. "If Roosevelt had lived …"

"It would have been different," Getty finished. "Yes. Maybe so. But he didn't." He sat beside January. "Cigarette?" He held out a pack, and January noticed the white wartime wrapper. He frowned.

"You haven't got a Camel?"

"Oh. Sorry."

"Oh well. That's all right." January took one of the Lucky Strikes, lit up. "That's awfully good news." He breathed out. "I never believed Truman would pardon me anyway, so mostly you've brought good news. Ha. They *missed*. You have no idea how much better that makes me feel."

"I think I do."

January smoked the cigarette.

"… So I'm a good American after all. I *am* a good American," he insisted, "no matter what Truman says."

"Yes," Getty replied, and coughed. "You're better than Truman any day."

"Better watch what you say, Father." He looked

into the eyes behind the glasses, and the expression he saw there gave him pause. Since the drop every look directed at him had been filled with contempt. He'd seen it so often during the court-martial that he'd learned to stop looking; and now he had to teach himself to see again. The priest looked at him as if he were … as if he were some kind of hero. That wasn't exactly right. But seeing it …

January would not live to see the years that followed, so he would never know what came of his action. He had given up casting his mind forward and imagining possibilities, because there was no point to it. His planning was ended. In any case he would not have been able to imagine the course of the post-war years. That the world would quickly become an armed camp pitched on the edge of atomic war, he might have predicted. But he never would have guessed that so many people would join a January Society. He would never know of the effect the Society had on Dewey during the Korean crisis, never know of the Society's successful campaign for the test ban treaty, and never learn that thanks in part to the Society and its allies, a treaty would be signed by the great powers that would reduce the number of atomic bombs year by year, until there were none left.

Frank January would never know any of that. But in that moment on his cot looking into the eyes of young Patrick Getty, he guessed an inkling of it—he felt, just for an instant, the impact on history.

And with that he relaxed. In his last week everyone who met him carried away the same impression, that of a calm, quiet man, angry at Truman and others, but in a withdrawn, matter-of-fact way. Patrick Getty, a strong force in the January Society ever after, said Janu-

THE LUCKY STRIKE | 57

ary was talkative for some time after he learned of the missed attack on Kokura. Then he became quieter and quieter, as the day approached. On the morning that they woke him at dawn to march him out to a hastily constructed execution shed, his MPs shook his hand. The priest was with him as he smoked a final cigarette, and they prepared to put the hood over his head. January looked at him calmly. "They load one of the guns with a blank cartridge, right?"

"Yes," Getty said.

"So each man in the squad can imagine he may not have shot me?"

"Yes. That's right."

A tight, unhumorous smile was January's last expression. He threw down the cigarette, ground it out, poked the priest in the arm. "But I *know*." Then the mask slipped back into place for good, making the hood redundant, and with a firm step January went to the wall. One might have said he was at peace.

A SENSITIVE DEPENDENCE
ON INIITIAL CONDITIONS

THE COVERING LAW MODEL of historical explanation states that an event is explained if it can be logically deduced from a set of initial conditions, and a set of general historical laws. These sets are the *explanans* and the event is the *explanandum*. The general laws are applied to the initial conditions, and the explanandum is shown to be the inevitable result. An explanation, in this model, has the same structure as a prediction.

On the morning of August 6th, 1945, Colonel Paul Tibbetts and his crew flew the *Enola Gay* from Tinian Island to Hiroshima, and dropped an atomic bomb on the city. Approximately a hundred thousand people died. Three days later, another crew dropped a bomb on the outskirts of Nagasaki. Approximately seventy thousand people died. The Japanese surrendered.

President Harry Truman, in consultation with his advisors, decided to drop the bombs. Why did he make these decisions? Because the Japanese had fiercely defended many islands in the South Pacific, and the cost of conquering them had been high. Kamikaze attacks had sunk many American ships, and it was said that the

Japanese would stage a gigantic kamikaze defense of the home islands. Estimated American casualties resulting from an invasion of the home islands ranged as high as a million men.

These were the conditions. General laws? Leaders want to end wars as quickly as possible, with a minimum of bloodshed. They also like to frighten potential postwar enemies. With the war in Europe ended, the Soviet Army stood ready to go wherever Stalin ordered it. No one could be sure where Stalin might want to go. An end to the Japanese war that frightened him would not be a bad thing.

But there were more conditions. The Japanese were defenseless in the air and at sea. American planes could bomb the home islands at will, and a total naval blockade of Japan was entirely possible. The Japanese civilian population was already starving; a blockade, combined with bombing of military sites, could very well have forced the Japanese leaders to surrender without an invasion.

But Truman and his advisors decided to drop the bombs. A complete explanation of the decision, omitted here due to considerations of length, would have to include an examination of the biographies of Truman, his advisors, the builders of the bomb, and the leaders of Japan and the Soviet Union; as well as a detailed analysis of the situation in Japan in 1945, and of American intelligence concerning that situation.

President Truman was re-elected in 1948, in an upset victory over Thomas Dewey. Two years later the United States went to war in Korea, to keep that country from being overrun by Communists supported by the Soviet Union and China. It was only one of many major wars in the second half of the twentieth century;

there were over sixty, and although none of them were nuclear, approximately fifty million people were killed.

Heisenberg's uncertainty principle says that we cannot simultaneously determine both the velocity and the position of a particle. This is not a function of human perception, but a basic property of the universe. Thus it will never be possible to achieve a deterministic prediction of the movement of all particles throughout spacetime. Quantum mechanics, which replaced classical mechanics as the best description of these events, can only predict the probabilities among a number of possible outcomes.

The covering law model of historical explanation asserts that there is no logical difference between historical explanation and scientific explanation. But the model's understanding of scientific explanation is based on classical mechanics. In quantum reality, the covering law model breaks down.

THE SUFFICIENT CONDITIONS MODEL of historical explanation is a modification of the covering law model; it states that if one can describe a set of initial conditions that are sufficient (but not necessary) for the event to occur, then the event can be said to be explained. Deduction from general law is not part of this model, which is descriptive rather than prescriptive, and "seeks only to achieve an acceptable degree of coherent narrative."

In July of 1945, Colonel Tibbetts was ordered to demonstrate his crew's ability to deliver an atomic weapon, by flying a test mission in the western Pacific. During the takeoff Tibbetts shut down both propellers on the right wing, to show that if this occurred during an armed takeoff, he would still be able to control the plane. The strain of this maneuver, however, caused the inboard left engine to fail, and in the emergency return to Tinian the *Enola Gay* crashed, killing everyone aboard.

A replacement crew was chosen from Tibbetts' squadron, and was sent to bomb Hiroshima on August 9th, 1945. During the run over Hiroshima the bombardier, Captain Frank January, deliberately delayed the release of the bomb, so that it missed Hiroshima by some ten miles. Another mission later that week encountered cloud cover, and missed Kokura by accident. January was court-martialed and executed for disobeying orders in battle. The Japanese having seen the explosions and evaluated the explosion sites, surrendered.

January decided to miss the target because: he had a visionary dream in which he saw the results of the bombing; he had not been in combat for over a year; he was convinced the war was over; he had been in London during the Blitz; he disliked his plane's pilot; he hated Paul Tibbetts; he was a loner, older than his fellow squadron members; he had read the Hornblower stories in the *Saturday Evening Post*; he once saw a truck crash into a car, and watched the truck driver in the aftermath; he was burned on the arm by stove oil when a child; he had an imagination.

The inboard left engine on the *Enola Gay* failed because a worker at the Wright manufacturing plant had failed to keep his welding torch flame on a weld for the required twenty seconds. He stopped three seconds too soon. He stopped three seconds too soon because he was tired. He was tired because the previous night he had stayed up late, drinking with friends.

In 1948, President Truman lost to Thomas Dewey in a close election that was slightly influenced by a political group called the January Society. The Korean conflict was settled by negotiation, and in February of

1956 a treaty was signed in Geneva, banning the use and manufacture of nuclear weapons.

Light behaves like either wave or particle, depending on how it is observed. The famous two-slit experiment, in which interference in wave patterns causes light shining through two slits in a partition to hit a screen in a pattern of light and dark bars, is a good example of this. Even when photons are sent at the slits one at a time, the pattern of light and dark bars still appears, implying that the single quantum of light is passing through both slits at the same time, creating an interference pattern with itself.

History is an interference pattern, says the covering law model. The conditions are particles; the laws are waves.

THE NECESSARY CONDITIONS MODEL states that historical explanation requires merely identifying the kind of historical event being explained, and then locating among its initial conditions some that seem necessary for the event to take place. No general laws of history can help; one can only locate more necessary conditions. As William Dray writes in *Laws and Explanation in History*, an explanandum is explained when we "can trace the course of events by which it came about."

Tibbetts and his crew died in a training flight crash, and the *Lucky Strike* was sent in the *Enola Gay's* place. The bombardier, Captain Frank January, after much frantic thought on the flight there, performed just as Tibbetts' bombardier would have, and dropped the bomb over the T-shaped Aioi Bridge in Hiroshima. Approximately a hundred thousand people died. Three days later Nagasaki was bombed. The Japanese surrendered. Truman was re-elected. The Korean War led to the Cold War, the assassination of Kennedy on November 22nd, 1963, the Vietnam War, the collapse of the Soviet bloc in the fall of 1989. Replacing one crew with another made no larger difference.

Richard Feynman's notion of a "sum over histories" proposes that a particle does not move from point A to point B by a single path, as in classical mechanics, but rather by every possible path within the wave. Two numbers describe these possible paths, one describing the size of the wave, the other the path's position in the crest-to-trough cycle. When Pauli's exclusion principle, which states that two particles cannot occupy the same position at the same velocity within the mathematical limits of the uncertainty principle, is applied to the sum over histories, it indicates that some possible paths cause interference patterns, and cancel each other out; other paths are phased in a reinforcing way, which makes their occurrence more probable.

Perhaps history has its own sum over histories, so that all possible histories resemble ours. Perhaps every possible bombardier chooses Hiroshima.

THE WEAK COVERING LAW model attempts to rescue the notion of general historical laws by relaxing their rigor, to the point where one can no longer deduce the explanandum from the explanans alone; the laws become not laws but tendencies, which help historians by providing "guiding threads" between events and their initial conditions. Thus the uncertainty principle is acknowledged, and the covering law model brought into the twentieth century.

But can any historical model explain the twentieth century? Tibbetts crashed, the *Lucky Strike* flew to Hiroshima, and Captain January chose to spare the city.

He was executed, the war ended, Dewey won the 1948 election; the Korean conflict was resolved by negotiation; and nuclear weapons were banned by treaty in February of 1956.

But go on. In November of 1956, conflict broke out in the Middle East between Egypt and Israel, and Britain and France quickly entered the conflict to protect their interests in the Suez Canal. President Dewey, soon to be replaced by President-elect Dwight Eisenhower, asked Britain and France to quit the conflict; his request was ignored. The war spread through the Middle East. In December the Soviet Army invaded West Germany. The United States declared war on the Soviet Union. China launched assaults in Indochina, and the Third World War was under way. Both the United States and the Soviet Union quickly assembled a number of atomic bombs, and in the first week of 1957, Jerusalem, Berlin, Bonn, Paris, London, Warsaw, Leningrad, Prague, Budapest, Beirut, Amman, Cairo, Moscow, Vladivostok, Tokyo, Peking, Los Angeles, Washington, D.C., and Princeton, New Jersey (hit by a bomb targeted for New York) were destroyed. Loss of life in that week and the year following was estimated at a hundred million people.

At normal energies, the strong nuclear force has a property called confinement, which binds quarks tightly together. At the high energies achieved in particle accelerators, however, the strong nuclear force becomes much weaker, allowing quarks and gluons to jet away almost like free particles. This property of dispersion at high energies is called "asymptotic freedom."

History is a particle accelerator. Energies are not always normal. We live in a condition of asymptotic freedom, and every history is possible. Each bombardier has to choose.

In *THE OPEN SOCIETY and Its Enemies* Karl Popper writes: "If two armies are equally well-led and well-armed, and one has an enormous numerical superiority, the other will never win." Popper made this proposition to demonstrate that any historical law with broad explanatory power would become so general as to be trivial. For the school of thought that agrees with him, there can be no covering laws.

In June of 1945, seven of the scientists who had worked on the Manhattan Project submitted a document called the Franck Report to the Scientific Panel of the Interim Committee, which was overseeing the progress of the bomb. The Franck Report called for a demonstration of the bomb before observers from many countries, including Japan. The Scientific Panel decided this was a possible option and passed the Report on to the Committee, which passed it on to the White House. "The Buck Stops Here." Truman read the Report and decided to invite James Franck, Leo Szilard, Niels Bohr, and Albert Einstein to the White House to discuss the issue. Final consultations included Oppenheimer, Secretary of War Stimson, and the military head of the Manhattan Project, General Leslie Groves. After a week's intense debate Truman instructed Stimson to contact the Japanese leadership and arrange a demonstration drop, to be made on one of the uninhabited islands in the Izu Shichito archipelago, south of Tokyo Bay. An atomic bomb was exploded on Udone Shima on August 24th, 1945; the mushroom cloud was visible from Tokyo. Films of the explosion were shown to Emperor Hirohito. The Emperor instructed his government to surrender, which it did on August 31st, one day before Truman had declared he was going to begin bombing Japanese cities.

Truman won the election of 1948. In 1950 North Korean troops invaded the south, until a series of six so-called Shima blasts, each closer to the north's advance forces, stopped them at the 38th parallel. In 1952 Adlai Stevenson became president, and appointed Leo Szilard the first presidential science advisor. In 1953 Stalin died, and in 1956 Szilard was sent to Moscow for a consultation with Khrushchev. This meeting led to the founding of the International Peace Brigade, which sent internationally integrated teams of young people to work in underdeveloped countries and in countries still recovering from World War Two. In 1960 John Kennedy was elected president, and he was succeeded in 1968 by his brother Robert. In 1976, in the wake of scandals in the administration, Richard Nixon was elected. At this point in time the postwar period is usually considered to have ended. The century itself came to a close without any further large wars. Though there had been a number of local conflicts, the existence of nuclear weapons had ended war as practiced in the first half of the century. In the second half, only about five million people died in war.

The great man theory considers particles; historical materialism considers waves. The wave/particle duality, confirmed many times by experiment, assures us that neither theory can be the complete truth. Neither theory will serve as the covering law.

THE DEFENDERS OF THE covering law model reply to its various critiques by stating that it is irrelevant whether historians actually use the model or not; the fact remains that they *should*. If they do not, then an event like "the bottle fell off the table" could be explained by either "the cat's tail brushed it," or "the cat looked at it cross-eyed," and there would be no basis for choosing between the two explanations. Historical explanation is not just a matter of the practice of historians, but of the nature of reality. And in reality, physical events are constrained by general laws—or if they are not laws, they are at least extraordinarily detailed descriptions of the links between an event and those that follow it, allowing predictions that, if not deterministically exact, are still accurate enough to give us enormous power over physical reality. That, for anyone but followers of David Hume, serves as law enough. And humans, as part of the stuff of the universe, are subject to the same physical laws that control all the rest of it. So it makes sense to seek a science of history, and to try to formulate some general historical laws.

What would these general laws look like? Some examples:

° If two armies are equally well-led and well-armed, and one has an enormous numerical superiority, the other will never win.

° A privileged group will never relinquish privilege voluntarily.

° Empires rise, flourish, fall and are replaced, in a cyclical pattern.

° A nation's fortunes depend on its success in war.

° A society's culture is determined by its economic system.

° Belief systems exist to disguise inequality.

° Lastly, unparalleled in both elegance and power, subsuming many of the examples listed above: power corrupts.

So there do seem to be some quite powerful laws of historical explanation. But consider another:

° For want of a nail, the battle was lost.

For instance: on July 29th, 1945, a nomad in Kirgiz walked out of his yurt and stepped on a butterfly. For lack of the butterfly flapping its wings, the wind in the area blew slightly less. A low pressure front therefore moved over east China more slowly than it would have. And so on August 6th, when the *Enola Gay* flew over Hiroshima, it was covered by ninety percent cloud cover, instead of fifty percent. Colonel Tibbetts flew to the secondary target, Nagasaki; it was also covered. The *Enola Gay* had little fuel left, but its crew was able to fly over Kokura on the way back to Tinian, and taking advantage of a break in the clouds, they dropped the bomb there. Ninety thousand people died in Kokura. The *Enola Gay* landed at Tinian with so little fuel left in its tanks that what remained "wouldn't have filled a cigarette lighter." On August 9th a second mission tried Hiroshima again, but the clouds were still there, and the mission eventually dropped the bomb on the less heavily clouded secondary target, Nagasaki, missing the city center and killing only twenty thousand people. The Japanese surrendered a week later.

On August 11th, 1945, a child named Ai Matsui was born in Hiroshima. In 1960 she began to speak in local meetings on many topics, including Hiroshima's special position in the world. Its citizens had escaped annihilation, she said, as if protected by some covering angel (or law); they had a responsibility to the dead of Kokura and Nagasaki, to represent them in the world of the living, to change the world for the good. The

Hiroshima Peace Party quickly grew to become the dominant political movement in Hiroshima, and then, in revulsion at the violence of the 1960s in Vietnam and elsewhere, all over Japan. In the 1970s the party became a worldwide movement, gaining the enthusiastic support of ex-President Kennedy, and President Babbitt. Young people from every country joined it as if experiencing a religious conversion. In 1983 Japan began its Asian Assistance League. One of its health care programs saved the life of a young woman in India, sick with malaria. The next year she had a child, a woman destined to become India's greatest leader. In 1987, the nation of Palestine raised its flag over the West Bank and parts of Jordan and Lebanon; a generation of camp children moved into homes. A child was born in Galilee. In 1990 Japan started its African Assistance League. The Hiroshima Peace Party had a billion members.

And so on; so that by July 29th, 2045, no human on Earth was the same as those who would have lived if the nomad in Kirgiz had not stepped on the butterfly a century before.

This phenomenon is known as the butterfly effect, and it is a serious problem for all other models of historical explanation; meaning trouble for you and for me. The scientific term for it is "sensitive dependence on initial conditions." It is an aspect of chaos theory first studied by the meteorologist Edward Lorenz, who, while running computer simulations of weather patterns, discovered that the slightest change in the initial conditions of the simulation would quickly lead to completely different weather.

o o o

So THE STRONG COVERING law model said that historical explanation should equal the rigor of scientific explanation. Then its defenders, bringing the model into the quantum world, conceded that predictions can never be anything but probabilistic at best. The explanandum was no longer deducible from the explanans; one could only suggest probabilities.

Now chaos theory has added new problems. And yet consider: Captain Frank January chose to miss Hiroshima. Ten years later, nuclear weapons were universally banned. Eleven years later, local conflicts in the Middle East erupted into general war, and nuclear weapons were quickly reassembled and used. For it is not easy to forget knowledge, once it is learned; symmetry T, which says that physical laws are the same no matter which way the time arrow is pointed, does not actually exist in nature. There is no going back.

And so by 1990, in this particular world, the bombed cities were rebuilt. The Western industrial nations were rich, the southern developing nations were poor. Multinational corporations ruled the world's economy. The Soviet bloc was falling apart. Gigantic sums of money were spent on armaments. By the year 2056, there was very little to distinguish this world from the one in which January had dropped the bomb, in which Tibbets had bombed Hiroshima, in which Tibbets had made a demonstration, in which Tibbets bombed Kokura.

Perhaps a sum over histories had bunched the probabilities. Is this likely? We don't know. We are particles, moving in a wave. The wave breaks. No math can predict which bubbles will appear where. But there is a sum over histories. Chaotic systems fall into patterns, following the pull of strange attractors. Linear chaotic figures look completely non-repetitive, but slice them into Poincaré sections and they reveal the simplest kinds of patterns. There is a tide, and we float in it; perhaps it is the flux of the cosmos itself; swim this way or that, the tide still carries us to the same destination. Perhaps.

So the covering law model is amended yet again. Explanations still require laws, but there are not laws for every event. The task of historical explanation becomes the act of making distinctions, between those parts of an event that can be explained by laws, and those that cannot. The component events that combine to create an explanandum are analyzed each in turn, and the historian then concentrates on the explicable components.

Paul Tibbetts flies toward Hiroshima. The nomad steps out of his yurt.

Lyapunov exponents are numbers that measure the conflicting effects of stretching, contracting, and folding in the phase space of an attractor. They set the topological parameters of unpredictability. An exponent greater than zero means stretching, so that each alternative history moves farther and farther apart as time passes. An exponent smaller than zero means contraction, so that alternatives tend to come back together. When the exponent equals zero, a periodic orbit results.

What is history's Lyapunov exponent? This is the law that no one can know.

Frank January flies toward Hiroshima. The nomad stops in his yurt.

It is said that the historian's task requires an imaginative reconstruction of the thinking of people who acted in the past, and of the circumstances in which they acted. "An explanation is said to be successful when the historian gets the sense of reliving the past which he is trying to explain."

You are flying toward Hiroshima. You are the bombardier. You have been given the assignment two days before. You know what the bomb will do. You do not know what you will do. You have to decide.

There are a hundred billion neurons in the brain. Some of the neurons have as many as eighty thousand synaptic endings. During thought, neurotransmitter chemicals flow across the synaptic clefts between one neuron's synaptic knobs and another's dendritic spines, reversing a slight electric charge, which passes on a signal. The passage of a signal often leaves changes in the synapses and dendrites along the way, forever altering the structure of the brain. This plasticity makes memory and learning possible. Brains are always growing; intensely in the first five years, then steadily thereafter.

At the moment of choice, then, signals fly through a neural network that has been shaped over a lifetime into a particular and unique structure. Some signals are conscious, others are not. According to Roger Penrose, during the process of decision quantum effects in the brain take over, allowing a great number of parallel and simultaneous computations to take place; the number could be extraordinarily large, 10 to the 21st power or more. Only at the intrusion of the "observation," that is to say a decision, do the parallel computations resolve back into a single conscious thought.

And in the act of deciding, the mind attempts the work of the historian: breaking the potential events down into their component parts, enumerating conditions, seeking covering laws that will allow a prediction of what will follow from the variety of possible choices.

Alternative futures branch like dendrites away from the present moment, shifting chaotically, pulled this way and that by attractors dimly perceived. Probable outcomes emerge from those less likely.

And then, in the myriad clefts of the quantum mind, a mystery: the choice is made. We have to choose, that is life in time. Some powerful selection process, perhaps aesthetic, perhaps moral, perhaps practical (survival of the thinker), shoves to consciousness those plans that seem safest, or most right, or most beautiful, we do not know; and the choice is made. And at the moment of this observation the great majority of alternatives disappear without trace, leaving us in our asymptotic freedom to act, uncertainly, in time's asymmetrical flow.

There are few covering laws. Initial conditions are never fully known. The butterfly may be on the wing, it may be crushed underfoot. You are flying toward Hiroshima.

"A REAL JOY TO BE HAD"
KIM STANLEY ROBINSON INTERVIEWED BY TERRY BISSON

David Hartwell once said that the Golden Age of Science Fiction is twelve. Was that true for you? What was your first literature?

I didn't know science fiction existed until I was eighteen; then I fell in pretty deeply. The first book I remember reading was *Huckleberry Finn*, and I still have that copy of the book with me, it has a gorgeous cover depicting Huck and Jim pulling a caught fish onto the raft, in vibrant colors. For years I pretended to be Huck Finn. My parents subscribed to the Scholastic book of the month club, and I read those when they came in the mail pretty much the day of arrival. I read everything that caught my eye at the library when I was a child, then as a teenager did the same, but became a fan of locked-room detective mysteries, chiefly John Dickson Carr but also Ellery Queen, and all the rest of that crowd from the 1930s. Then just as I was leaving for college I ran into the science fiction section at the library, all the books with their rocketship-and-radiation signs on the spine, and that was very exciting. In college I majored in history and literature, and on the side majored in science fiction, absorbing the New Wave pretty much as it happened.

Did your parents read to you as a kid? Did anyone? Do you read to your kids?

Yes, my mom read to my brother and me at bedtime, and then I read on by myself with a flashlight. I read at bedtime to my older son throughout his childhood and youth at home (my wife read to the younger son) and we made our way through all of Joan Aiken, the entire Patrick O'Brian sequence, many kids' books I remembered from my childhood and found in used bookstores, and many more. Now that my son is off to college I miss that very much, and have tried to horn in on the younger son, but no luck. It's sad to be done, and I have to say, along with everything else, it certainly helped me with my public readings of my own work. My mouth just got stronger and more versatile.

Do you touch type? Do you write on a computer? I hear you and Karen Fowler like to write in cafes. What's that about?

Yes, I touch type, and I can go really fast, although not accurately. I write by hand in a notebook, and then on a laptop for fiction. I'm trying to work outdoors now, in the shade of my front courtyard, it's very nice. Being outdoors helps a lot.

I wrote in cafes for many years, and I liked that too; I liked seeing the faces, which often became characters' faces, and I liked hearing the voices around me, I think it helped with dialogue, and made my writing even more a matter of channeling a community. Karen

Fowler joined me in this at several cafes downtown, all of which died, we hope not from our presence, although we may have killed three. It was good to meet with someone going through the same issues, it was a kind of solidarity and also a bit of policing, in that there was someone to meet at a certain time, who would then be watching in a way. It was a great addition to a friendship. But now Karen has moved, and on my own I'm finding I like my courtyard better than any of the cafes left in town. I thought I was getting tired of writing, before, but now I realize I was only tired of spending so much time indoors sitting around. When it's outdoors it feels completely different.

Were you ever tempted to keep a journal? Did you give in?

Tempted maybe, but I never gave in. Except in this way; long ago I started filling out a Sierra Club weekly calendar, which has only a narrow space for every day, with a week per page—you know the type. So every day could only be given a few sentences at most, basically a bare description of what that day held, very minimal. I now have twenty-three years of those filled out, and my wife and I have a game where I keep the ones from ten and twenty years before on the bed table under the new one, and I tell her what we were doing ten years ago and twenty years ago on that day. It is a way of placing us in time and our own lives that is very interesting, and we get some good laughs and often some groans. Twenty years ago we were young, without children, living in Europe, dashing all over in trains and planes, seeing romantic cities like Venice and Edinburgh, etc; in the present, going to work and buying groceries, the entry for every day almost identical. But oh well. It's also a very interesting test of the memory, because sometimes we won't remember events or even people, but other times a single sentence will bring back a very full memory of an event; and that memory, there in the brain waiting, would never, never have come back to us if we hadn't had the spur of the sentence in the journal. So, as memories may need to be remembered to hold fast as structures in the brain, this is a good thing in itself. But we've become convinced that an evolutionary accident has left us in the curious state of having brains that can remember huge, huge amounts of incident; but we have no good recall mechanisms in us to go back and get them, so they sit there as knots or configurations of synapses, doing nothing but waiting. Very strange.

As for journals, I love the journals of Henry David Thoreau and Virginia Woolf, and often feel they are the whole story as far as literature goes; they are novels written as first person hyperrealist accounts of a single consciousness, say. And we don't have any other novels that come even close to doing what they do as far as getting inside the head of another human being—except possibly for Proust's novel. So they are considerable works of literature in that sense and I often wonder if a journal would be the best way to go if you were intent to do this particular thing, which it seems to me most literature does indeed want to do. But neither Woolf nor Thoreau had kids. There's a time problem here, and also it takes a certain mentality to keep at it year after year, which is what is required. Also, with both of them, when really bad things happened, their journals went silent, usually for months and sometimes for years. So there seems to be some kind of problem there with what the journal can actually face up to, as a form. Maybe.

I know that you write and publish poetry. Have you published outside the SF field? Have you published fiction outside the field?

No, all my poetry is stuck inside my stories and books. It helps me to think of my poems as being by someone else. And all my fiction has been published in SF magazines or books, although sometimes brought out as "general fiction," by my publisher, but booksellers know which section to put it in after it's off the front tables.

Are there special "chops" for writing SF? Are there ways in which SF is less demanding?

I don't know, I guess there are some techniques particular to SF, maybe the ways in which the future background is conveyed, or something like that. I can't imagine it's less demanding than any other kind of fiction, it feels about as demanding as I can handle, anyway. My near future and my farther future stories feel about the same in terms of writing, although I will say that when I came back from years on Mars to write about Antarctica, it was a huge relief to have other people making up the culture for me, rather than trying to do it all myself. In that sense I think SF is a bit harder. But it's all hard, and none of it is "realism," so I think distinctions here are very fuzzy.

What part of the process of writing fiction do you like best? Least? Is there a process to writing fiction?

I like the writing. These days I write only novels, and I like most the last three to six months of writing a novel, when I bear down and really go at it like a maniac. There is a real joy to be had in submitting to a task like a madman. It feels like things are coming together, and the process is one of identifying problems and then solving them on the spot, and then moving on. So there is a problem-solving aspect to it that reminds me of hiking cross country in Sierra, where every step is a decision, like every word coming up in a sentence. You get into a flow and then it's problem, solution, problem, solution, and that goes on at a smooth good pace for a long time, and at the end you're somewhere else. Often when in this flow state I will have a couple of hours pass and it feels like only about fifteen minutes have passed, and that I take it is the blessed state, the Zen state, prayer, what have you. Writing as hiking a prayer.

The part I like least. . . . Well, first draft when faced with a hard idea can be tough. It makes you feel stupid. But I have learned to ignore that and grind on, and so it's not so bad once you get in the habit. I don't much like dealing with editorial comments, but truthfully, my editors now are so good that that part is not so unpleasant either, because it's helping the book and that always feels good. I like readings. I don't like the wasted time associated with business travel, but this is not a very bad thing either. I guess I mostly like all of it. I don't like people telling me what fiction is or is not, in the sense of what I can or cannot do (see below).

Do you research and then write, or do the two overlap?

I usually research as I am writing, on a need to know basis. If I did my research first, I would never get started writing. I call this the Coleridge Problem, because he listed all the things he would need to learn before he could write his epic poem, and he never wrote his epic poem. And I find the research is so much more effective when it is specifically to support a particular scene or chapter. So in the *Mars* books, the *Years of Rice and Salt*, and the climate books, I researched as I wrote and it worked very well to suggest to me what the scenes needed, or better, how they could be extended or made even more interesting. It's a good stimulus to fiction, researching on the fly.

Where did the idea of Years of Rice and Salt *come from? That's got to be one of the great UNDISCOVERED high concept ideas of SF. Mostly we recycle old ones (apocalypse, first contact, etc). Was that a 'eureka' moment, or did it just leak in from somewhere?*

Thanks, I like that idea myself. It came to me in the late 70s, and it was indeed a kind of AH HA moment, in that I was thinking about alternative histories, wanting ideas, and thought of the one for "The Lucky Strike" too, and looking over the alternative histories I decided what was needed was the most major change you could think of, that did not simply change the game so much that it wiped away everything. Because you want comparison. So that Harry Harrison's novel in which dinosaurs evolve to high intelligence instead of mammals, is an alternative history in a way, but not— useless as such, because the comparisons are invalidated by the fact that the difference there is too huge to be able to play the game. So I was thinking, well what would be the biggest change that would still work in terms of comparison to our history, and it seemed to me that Europe's conquering the world was so big that if it hadn't happened—and then it hit me, and I said *Wow* and ran to write it down quick before I forgot it and ended up wandering around moaning saying I had a good idea, I had a good idea but I can't remember it now, it won't come back—which has sometimes happened to me.

So, once I had the idea, I knew I couldn't write it, that what it implied was beyond what I was capable of expressing. I wondered if I would ever be capable of such a thing (I have a couple of good ideas I've never written because I can't think how to yet), but after the Mars novels I figured I had worked out the method, and I was feeling bold. I'm glad I wrote it when I did; I don't know if I have the brain cells for it now. Although that's partly that book's fault, because I blew out some fuses writing that one that were never replaced.

Antarctica. You were there. Was that scary, or just fun?

It was fun. I was having fun every waking moment, and I seldom slept. It was so beautiful, and alien; like being on another planet.

I did have one scary twenty minutes, when we were in a Kiwi helicopter, pilot about twenty-eight, a real vet, and co-pilot about twenty-four, and we were trying to fly around Ross Island's north end to get from Cape Crozier back to McMurdo, rather than taking the straight route around the south end; and we were flying toward a cloud bank and the co-pilot, flying, said to the pilot, "you don't want me to fly into that do you?" and there was a silence of about ten seconds before the pilot said "No," and we turned around. But then we had about twenty minutes flying back toward Cape Crozier, where it wasn't clear that the winds would allow us to land. Under us was black water with orca pods visible (very cool before) and the very steep snowy side of Ross Island. And there are a fair number of crashed helicopters still half-buried in snow all over Ross Island and the dry valleys, so we knew what could happen. In the end the co-pilot stuck the landing straight into the wind at Cape Crozier and we retired to the penguin scientists' hut there and hung out for twenty-four hours until the winds died down.

Other than that, it was heaven. I would love to go back.

You're pretty good at landscape. What's that about? Is it a fictional skill or something else entirely? You're also pretty good at erotic scenes.

Thanks. I like landscapes and think they are worth some sentences to describe. Also, I've seen some landscapes and paid attention when in them, so that I feel I can bring something new to the page when I write them, something I saw myself rather than read in a book. There are a fair number of writers who write down only things they have learned in books, and in their personal relationships. They think that being nifty or tasteful with the word combinations is enough to make it good writing, but I'm not so sure. I think new perceptions out of the world are better. So this is something I can bring.

As for erotic scenes, I decided long ago that I wasn't going to put violence in my stories just to jazz up the plots, like Hollywood and TV—that that was fake too, it was all out of books and TV and movies, and the writers didn't know what they were talking about, and if I tried I wouldn't either. It's guesswork, it's lazy, it's a cheat. So, but fiction these days and maybe always is pretty reliant on sex and violence, and so without violence, that left sex. Everyone's an expert there, so the test for writing about it is finding ways to make it sexy. That's not easy, but it is fun to try.

Someone once described your Mars *books as an infodump tunneled by narrative moles. I think it was a compliment. What do you think?*

No, not a compliment. I reject the word "infodump" categorically—that's a smartass word out of the cyberpunks' workshop culture, them thinking that they knew how fiction works, as if it were a tinker toy they could disassemble and label superciliously, as if they knew what they were doing. Not true in any way. I reject "expository lump" also, which is another way of saying it. All these are attacks on the idea that fiction can have any kind of writing included in it. It's an attempt to say "fiction can only be stage business" which is a stupid position I abhor and find all too common in responses on amazon.com and the like. All these people who think they know what fiction is, where do they come from? I've been writing it for thirty years and I don't know what it is, but what I do know is that the novel in particular is a very big and flexible form, and I say, or sing: Don't fence me in!

I say, what's interesting is whatever you can make interesting. And the world is interesting beyond our silly stage business. So "exposition" creeps in. What is it anyway? It's just another kind of narrative. One thing I believe: it's all narrative. Once you get out of the phone book anyway, it's all narrative.

And in science fiction, you need some science sometimes; and science is expository; and so science fiction without exposition is like science fiction without science, and we have a lot of that, but it's not good. So the word "infodump" is like a red flag to me, it's a Thought Police command saying "Dumb it down, quit talking about the world, people don't have attention spans, blah blah blah blah." No. I say, go read *Moby Dick*, Dostoevsky, Garcia Marquez, Jameson, Bahktin, Joyce, Sterne—learn a little bit about what fiction can do and come back to me when you're done. That would be never and I could go about my work in peace.

But I thought you liked infodumps.

I do! But let's call them something different and also think of them differently. Think about all writing as narrative, because it is (outside the phone book and other such places). Scientific abstracts, *TV Guide* summaries, all writing has information that traverses time in the telling and in reality too, so it's ALL narrative. So, okay, some of these omnipresent stories are about us, and some of these stories are about the rest of the world. And what I think the people who speak of "expository lumps" or the smart-asses who reduced that to "infodumps" are saying is, you can only talk about us. The proper study of mankind is man (Pope) etc., etc., well, that's just silly. Why be so narcissistic? There are many, many stories that are extremely interesting that don't happen to be about us. That's what science is saying, often, and that's what I'm saying in my science fiction. So, my *Mars* novels are a narrative, the story never stops for even a sentence, even in the list of tools that goes on for two pages, it's just that sometimes it's the story of the rocks and the tools and the weather, and sometimes it's the story of the people there in interaction with all that. I know it reads a bit differently and freaks some people out, but I can see others like it as well. Even some of the people freaked out read on, irritated and mystified.

What do you think of the current state of Earth's Mars enterprise?

Well, the robot landers are sending back some fantastic photos. And the orbiting satellites. A balloon floating at low altitude and taking good photos and moving images would be mind-boggling too. As for human landings, those would be exciting, but they seem a long way off; I don't know if we are going to see them in our lifetimes. But I don't think there's any hurry there. I'm not in the group who says we have to go there fast to save our civilization, etc. I don't believe it's true. We need a healthy Earth and a sustainable civilization, and the Mars project will come. So it may be some time.

How come you only drive Fords?

Ha, well, my dad worked for Ford Aerospace and so he got to buy Fords at dealer cost or lower, and his family too, and this was therefore something he could do for us. I've driven a Cortina, an Escort station wagon, and a Focus station wagon, those have been good cars, and my wife has driven two Tauruses, we won't talk about those. I want my next car to be a little electric station wagon that I can sleep in the back and fit in my bikes and bales of hay. If Ford makes one, fine. If not I may be off somewhere else.

You're a big supporter of Clarion, the science fiction "boot-camp" workshop. Why?

I'm a big Clarion supporter because I tried to express my thanks to a dead person. Maybe not the best idea.

Clarion gave me a six-week party and a group of good friends, a cohort, a block party in the small town that is science fiction. It gave me tangible evidence that I was serious about becoming a writer, and taught me a lot of craft points, some of which I agreed with, others not. It gave me some time with six fine writers and people (Delany, Wolfe, Zelazny, Haldeman, Knight and Wilhelm) whom I've read with intense interest and pleasure ever since.

What do you think of the current MFA-in-writing boom? Do you think working in a commercial field (like SF) sharpens or dilutes a writer's vision?

I think getting an MFA in creative writing is a bad idea. If you want a graduate degree to help get a job, then the PhD is stronger and gives you more options. With an MFA you need also publishing credits to get a job, so it is not sufficient in itself, as a PhD is, and it only gives you a chance at teaching writing anyway, not all literature. So it's weak in that sense. If you are going for that MFA in order to learn more about writing, I'd say any other graduate degree will give you more raw material for your writing, while you can teach yourself writing on your own; you will be anyway.

I don't know what working in a commercial field does to a writer's vision. A lot of the effect must be unconscious. Ultimately you seem to be saying, does the desire for readers change what you write? Surely it must. But isn't the desire for readers pretty basic to writing? So, maybe it sharpens your vision, in those terms.

Have you ever thought of yourself as part of a "school" in SF? Did it last? Was it fun?

Oh I hate all literary schools, not just the ones in SF but everywhere. In science fiction they are particularly small and stupid: marketing ploys, herding instincts, white guys wishing they were back in high school and were the tough guys smoking cigarettes out in the parking lot—that's a deeply stupid thing to wish for—gee, I wish I was back in high school. Sorry, but no.

I was called "literary science fiction" for a while, that's the kiss of death in terms of sales, then I was a victim of certain cyberpunks' need to have somebody to mug to show they were punks, that was fine, but a "school" was invented to "oppose" them in a rumble like the Sharks and the Jets, so then I was a "humanist," that was dumb; then I wrote the *Mars* books and I was suddenly "hard SF," but hard sf is only hard in its attitude toward the poor, in other words right wing, so that didn't seem to fit very well, even though I talked about technology. Now people have given up. Sometimes I am called "utopian SF" but that could not be a school, as there is only you and me and Ursula in it: a study group more than a school. Well, I just don't believe in them. I believe in science fiction, which is a kind of small town in literature, not highly regarded by big city people, but I like it, and I like the big city too. The whole point is to be as idiosyncratic as possible, the town madman. Although in our town that's a tough label to earn.

Were you ever close to any of the "old-timers" in SF? Which ones? What did you get from them?

Not really close, but I loved the several interactions I had with Jack Williamson, one of the kindest, smartest people in writing, modest but incisive. He published science fiction from 1928 to 2008—isn't that eighty years? I'm having trouble believing my math. Anyway he was great.

I've met Asimov and Bradbury, and talked with Clarke on the phone, and they are all generous friendly people. I guess I get from them the sense that the community is a real community, that the people in it function like neighbors in a small town, helpful to the young people.

Your first big trilogy was the Orange County (Wild Shore) series. Did you feel you owed that to your birthplace or was it because Orange County California somehow concentrates all the tendencies good and bad in modern America?

That trilogy is called *Three Californias*, as the handsome Tor trade paperbacks say. I guess it was a little of both. I wanted to ground some of my science fiction in my actual home town, and I also felt like I was the beneficiary of a lucky coincidence, in that my home town seemed to me to represent some kind of end case for America, some kind of future already here for the rest of the country to witness and hopefully avoid following. I'm not sure that was a true perception, but it had to do with the westward movement in American history, and the fact that when people reached the Pacific there was no where else to go, so the leading edge of malcontents and dreamers was stuck there and had to make something of it. LA is the big exemplar of how that can go wrong, San Francisco how it can go right, and Orange County is like the purest expression of LA. And in my time it was so beautiful, then it was so destroyed, and it was so drugged out; it seemed a good spot to talk about America, so I used it. It still feels like a lucky thing, and I think it was fundamental to me becoming a science fiction writer in the first place. When I ran into science fiction at age eighteen, I said, Oh I recognize this, this is home, this is Orange County.

My favorite of that series is Pacific Edge, *the Utopia. What's yours? Are there any particular problems in writing a Utopia?*

My favorite is *The Gold Coast*, for personal reasons, but I think *Pacific Edge* is more important to us now. Anyone can do a dystopia these days just by making a collage of newspaper headlines, but utopias are hard, and important, because we need to imagine what it might be like if we did things well enough to say to our kids, we did our best, this is about as good as it was when it was handed to us, take care of it and do better. Some kind of narrative vision of what we're trying for as a civilization. It's a slim tradition since More invented the word, but a very interesting one, and at certain points important: the Bellamy clubs after Edward Bellamy's *Looking Back from the Year 2000* had a big impact on the Progressive movement in American politics, and H.G. Wells's stubborn persistence in writing utopias over about fifty years (not his big sellers) conveyed the vision that got turned into the postwar order of social security and some kind of government-by-meritocracy. So utopias have had effects in the real world.

More recently I think *Ecotopia* by Callenbach had a big impact on how the hippie generation tried to live in the years after, building families and communities.

There are a lot of problems in writing utopias, but they can be opportunities. The usual objections, that they must be boring, are often political attacks, or ignorant repeating of a line, or another way of saying "No expository lumps please, it has to be about me." The political attacks are interesting to parse. "Utopia would be boring because there would be no conflicts, history would stop, there would be no great art, no drama, no magnificence." This is always said by white people with a full belly. My feeling is that if they were hungry and sick and living in a cardboard shack they would be more willing to give utopia a try. And if we did achieve a just and sustainable world civilization, I'm confident there would still be enough drama, as I tried to show in *Pacific Edge*. There would still be love lost, there would still be death. That would be enough. The horribleness of unnecessary tragedy may be lessened and the people who like that kind of thing would have to deal with a reduction in their supply of drama.

So, the writing of utopia comes down to figuring out ways of talking about just these issues in an interesting way; how tenuous it would be, how fragile, how much a tightrope walk and a work in progress. That along with the usual science fiction problem of handling exposition. It could be done, and I wish it were being done more often.

Your two early "stand-alones" anticipated some later themes: super-longevity and terraforming in Icehenge. *And in* Memory of Whiteness *the exploration of ten-dimensional space. What keeps you coming back to these themes?*

I like the super-longevity theme because I'd like to live five hundred years, and also from time to time when I think back on my past, it feels like I've lived five hundred years, so it works as both wish and metaphor. And the whole thrust of medicine leads toward that wish, I think. So it's good science fiction. Same with terraforming Mars, which is very achievable, and even the idea of terraforming other places is interesting to contemplate. It's also a good metaphor for what we now have to do here on Earth, for the rest of human time. As for ten-dimensional space, physicists keep coming back to it, ever since Kaluza and Klein in the twenties, and I keep thinking, what the heck can it mean? It seems to stand in for all the deep weirdness of modern physics and what they are saying about this world we live in, but apparently don't see very well. Also, if you have foolishly taken on a time travel story, it's the only way to make it look like it makes sense.

Are you sorry Pluto is no longer a planet?

No, not at all. I think it's a good lesson in words.

These books came out at about the same time as the Three Californias. *Were they written earlier? Or in between?*

I somewhat wrote them all at once, or overlapping through those years. It went something like, *Icehenge* part 3, *Memory of Whiteness* early drafts, *Icehenge* part 1, *Wild Shore, Icehenge* part 2, and *Memory of Whiteness* final drafts. *The Gold Coast* and *Pacific Edge* came later.

You once said that a writer had to perch on a three-legged stool. I think (!) you meant that you had three readerships: the SF community, the science community, and the more "literary" types. Does that still work for you?

Yes, I think that might describe the three parts of my adult audience, although I think college students and high school students form a group as big as any of these three. Also, leftists, environmentalists, and wilderness people. I like all these readerships very much, indeed I am deeply grateful to them, as providing me my career and my sense of myself as a writer. I'm not a writer without them. So, thinking of the SF community as my home town, I guess I think of the "literary" community as another small town, with pretensions, while scientists are the real big city, but they tend to act like a big city, in that they don't know each other and usually don't read fiction; so word of mouth doesn't work as well there as in the other communities. Younger readers use word of mouth and also listen to their teachers, a bit, so they are crucial. Getting word to people who would enjoy my books if they were to give them a try; this is the big problem, and ultimately it comes down to word of mouth. So again I depend on my readership. It's a real dependency!

You are firmly ensconced in a genre (SF). Many writers regard that as a trap, and others as an opportunity. How do you see it? Is working in a field with a developed, opinionated and rambunctious "fandom" a blessing or a curse?

It's the home town. It's a floor and a ceiling, in some respects. I love the genre and the community, but want readers who don't usually think of themselves as

SF readers to give me a try, as they have in the past for Bradbury, Asimov, Frank Herbert, Ursula Le Guin, and so on.

These days there seems to be a lot of permeability. Chabon's *The Yiddish Policeman's Union* was a great SF novel, an alternative history, but that's SF too, and it was widely read and enjoyed by people. Maybe Philip K. Dick's takeover of the movies helped break down part of the barriers.

Anyway there is no reason to pretend it's a ghetto and we are oppressed artists that the world won't give a break. In the 1950s that was true and drove many writers mad. Now to hold that position (which some do) would be only a confession that you'd rather be a big fish in a little pond than swim in the big ocean. I like the ocean, but I love SF too. And really, to have a literary community as a kind of feedback amp on stage, loudly talking back to you and ready to talk at any moment—any writer is lucky to have that. The solitude and alienation of many writers from their audiences strikes me as sad. It's solitary enough as it is, in the daily work.

You wrote your PhD thesis on PK Dick. Did you ever meet him? He seems to be on the verge of replacing Asimov as the most familiar SF name. How do you think he would fit into today's market?

I met PKD once in a hallway at Cal State Fullerton, where we both had come to see a lecture by Harlan Ellison. PKD rose to his feet during the Q and A after the reading to thank Ellison publicly for raising the level of respect for SF in the general culture; PKD really felt the put-downs of the literary culture back in the 1950s. (This was 1973). Afterwards in the hall I said to him how much I had enjoyed his novel *Galactic Pot-Healer*. He looked at me like I was insane. He may or may not have said thank you, or anything. But I'm glad I did it.

I guess he is "the SF writer" in American culture now. I think it's fitting; we live in a PKD reality in a lot of ways, crazier than Asimov's vision. So many of PKD's visions now look prescient and like perfect metaphors for life now. He had a big gift that way.

Many of his novels were written in two weeks on speed, and it shows. In today's market (especially if all his movies had been made) he would have been able to afford to slow down. He was skillful; if he had to start in today's market, he would do okay; if he were still alive and had his real start, he would be huge. And his books would be very interesting no matter what. He was a good novelist.

Tom Disch once said that all SF is really fantasy. Was that just Disch or is there a grain of truth in it?

I think it's a little of both. Imagining the future; that has to be fantasy, by some definitions. But some of these fantasies of the future can conform to what we think is physically possible, and that would be science fiction, by my lights. A fictional future, meaning there is a historical connection explained or implied between that future and our now, with whatever's in that future sounding physically possible. This would rule out faster-than-light travel and time travel, which are in science fiction all the time, so maybe that's what Disch meant. But you can dispense with those and have a "real" SF I think.

Disch got very angry at the SF community, as his home town that had somehow rejected him despite his great work. Too bad. It's not the whole of his story, by any means, but part of it. I like many of his books and stories, but distrust anything he said about SF. He was too angry.

SF writers are always complaining about the state of publishing. What do you think would be the proper role of SF in a proper publishing world? Would there be genres or categories at all?

I don't know! That's a real alternative history. If there were no genres or categories, people might be more open to trying new things. That would be good. I'd love to try it. But it's not the world we have. Going forward from now, I guess I think every science fiction section in every bookstore should have a sign saying "Science Fiction—You Live Here, why not read about it?" or "Science Fiction, the Most Real Part of This Store" or something like that. Something to remind people of reality, which is that we are all stuck in a big SF novel now, and there's no escape; might as well accept it and dive in.

You are a minimalist in your long-distance Sierra treks: superlight pack, no tent floor, no poles even, no stove, just a pellet and stones. Does any of this apply to your writing? I know you cover a lot of ground....

No, in my writing I am more of a maximalist. I'll try anything, include anything; I don't think I have a method that works for everything, as the literary minimalists seemed to think.

I hike ultra-light in the Sierras because I can be just as comfortable in camp, while suffering less on trail when I've got my house on my back. It's a version of the technological sublime. It's very high-tech, it's not a Luddite thing at all. My mountain experiences are philosophically complicated, but they feel like bliss to me, like devotion or prayer in a religion, so I do it and enjoy it, and at home like to think about it too. But I will spare you my ultra-light ultra-cool gear list and technique.

If you were to take up a trade, what would it be? If you could play music what would you play? Do you listen to music when you work?

I like working with stone and would love to be an artsy drywall mason, like Andy Goldsworthy or the more local and practical drywall stone artists in New England. I'd be good I think: it's like novel writing, the pattern work, and I like stones.

I play the trumpet and would love to play like Louis Armstrong or Clifford Brown, but good luck with that! Every trumpet player says that, but it can't be done.

I do listen to music when I work, mostly music without lyrics in English, and lots of different kinds. I pick the music to fit the mood I want for the scene I'm writing. I don't really hear it while working, but I'm sure it has an effect.

Who are your favorite poets? Who do you read for fun?

I like Gary Snyder and W.S. Merwin among living poets, also many more American poets, especially Stevens, William Bronk, Rexroth, and the whole 20th century American tradition, also the English romantics, and the Elizabethans. I like poetry. I read it for fun, usually one poem last thing before sleeping; before that I've read a half hour or so in a novel. I'm always reading a novel, I love novels, and I try to read widely, try new writers. Non-fiction I read for work or at meals.

*Your recent "Global Warming" trilogy (*40 Signs of Rain; 50 Degrees Below; 60 Days and Counting*) was about global warming—which leads to a deep freeze! What do you think of Obama's "green" agenda? Is it headed in the right directions?*

Climate change will mostly be warming, but that will add such energy to the world system that the turbulence will lead to areas of greater cold in winter, as well as more severe storms, etc. So I followed a scenario that describes the "abrupt climate change" that the scientists have found in the historical record, that results when the Gulf Stream is shut down at its north end by too much fresh water flooding the far north Atlantic. That could happen with Greenland melting, though now they think it is lower probability than when I wrote (oh well).

I like Obama's green agenda and hope his whole team and everyone jumps on board and pushes it as hard as possible.

On thing happening is that the Republican Party in the USA has decided to fight the idea of climate change (polls and studies show the shift over the first decade of this century, in terms of the leadership turning against it and the rank and file following) which is like the Catholic Church denying the Earth went around the sun in Galileo's time; a big mistake they are going to crawl away from later and pretend never happened. And here the damage could be worse, because we need to act now.

What's been set up and is playing out now is a Huge World Historical Battle between science and capitalism. Science is insisting more emphatically every day that this is a real and present danger. Capitalism is saying it isn't, because if it were true it would mean more government control of economies, more social justice (as a climate stabilization technique) and so on. These are the two big players in our civilization, so I say, be aware, watch the heavyweights go at it, and back science every chance you get. I speak to all fellow leftists around the world: science is now a leftism, and thank God; but capitalism is very very strong. So it's a dangerous moment. People who like their history dramatic and non-utopian should be pleased.

Have you done any audio books? What about film or TV?

I haven't read for my audio books, but several of my books are on audio books. No film or TV, though the AMC channel is in the early stages of developing *Red Mars* as a TV series. That would be nice but it's a long way from happening right now.

Where does Short Sharp Shock *fit into your canon? Is it fantasy?*

I think of it as my version of fantasy, what I think fantasy ought to be: strange, new imagery, a possible science fiction explanation (science fantasy is that subgenre of science fiction set so far in the future that it looks like fantasy, done well by Vance and Wolfe). My vision of fantasy does not seem to have been picked up on, but what can you do.

I wrote it when our first kid was born and I was not sleeping much nor writing much. I decided I would write no matter what, and it might be best to try a dream narrative. It was right before *Red Mars*, and I knew I would be spending years on a very rational, historical project, so I thought it might be good to discharge some craziness in the system before I embarked on that. I very much enjoyed working on *Short Sharp Shock* and I appreciate my publisher Bantam keeping it in print.

You wrote a wonderful book about Everest, Escape from Kathmandu. *Was any of that based on personal experience? Was your prediction about Mallory and Irvine based on secret info just luck?*

Yes, a lot of it was based on the trek my wife and I took in Nepal in 1985. We ran into Jimmy Carter, laughed hard every day, enjoyed our Sherpa handlers, who took care of us like pets, and loved the country and the mountains. I'd like to go back and write a book called *Return to Kathmandu*, using George and Freds again. There have been so many changes in the twenty-three years since, but I bet much is the same too. I got some calls right, about the revolutionary forces, and also about the Mallory find on the north side of Everest. That was just luck, but I could see how it would be possible.

How would you describe your politics? What was your relationship to the anti-war movement and the political currents of the 60s? Were you an activist? Are you today?

I call myself an American leftist and try to point to all the left activities in American history as a tradition of resistance, activism and successes. Indeed today I read in the paper about the election of a leftist president in El Salvador, and the chant was "The left—united—will never be defeated." Very nice thought, especially since the divisions in and among the leftisms have been such a problem. Those are so often what Freud called "the narcissism of small differences" and that is an important concept everyone should study....

I was at UCSD during the anti-war movement, or I should say, after 1970. In the 1960s I was in Orange County in high school and it might as well have been 1953, except for the news of distant places. At UCSD things were more up-to-date, and I transitioned into anti-war sentiments as part of my group cohort feeling, and my draft number (89). I saw Marcuse and Angela Davis speak at a rally at the gym, and gathered on campus a couple times, but I was a follower. By the time I had ideas of my own the war was over.

I am only an activist today in the local politics of my town, Davis, California, where I am trying to fight a real estate development proposed by the university. It's pretty draining and uphill work. I think of my writing as an activism, and we give financial support to a lot of activist causes.

You were a student of the famed post-modernist Fredric Jameson. How has he influenced your work?

Famous Marxist Fredric Jameson, you mean. What he managed was to rearrange everyone's definition of postmodernism from a fashion or a style, to a period in the history of capital and the world. So that was quite an accomplishment. And his persistence over the years has given a kind of lens for leftists and everyone else to understand modern history in Marxist terms. So, that has been a major influence on everyone, I think, even if for most people it is indirect.

For me it was direct. Fred is very educational in person, a great teacher, and after our time together at UCSD I kept reading him, and by reading all his work gave myself a good ground for understanding world history and our moment today. That's a great thing for a novelist to have. I've stayed in touch too and he is a good person to know, perpetually interesting.

I understand that you live in a utopian community. How does that work? Is it pre or post modern?

A little of both I guess. The model is an English village really; about eighty acres, a lot of it owned in common, so there is a "commons" and no fences except around little courtyards. There are a lot of vegetable gardens, and the landscaping is edible, meaning lots of fruits, grapes and nuts.

It's really just a tweaking of suburban design, but a really good one. Energy mattered to the designers and we burn about 40 percent the energy of an ordinary suburban neighborhood of the same size. That's still a lot, but it's an improvement. If every suburb since this one was built (1980 or so) would have followed its lead, we would have much less craziness in America; because the standard suburb is bad for sanity. But that didn't happen, so for the 1,000 people who live here it's a kind of pocket utopia. Not the solution, but a nice place to live right now, and it could suggest aspects of a long-term solution. It's been a real blessing to live here.

You gave one of the Google talks. Was that cool or what? What did you tell them?

It was a lot of fun. The Google people were great, and their free cafeteria is out of this world. They put the talk online so you can find it on YouTube. It was my first Power Point talk ever, so that was a bit clunky, but fun. It was configured as a talk to the Googlers, telling Google what it could do to fight climate change and enact utopia. I'm not sure the folks at Google.org (their charitable/activist foundation) were listening, but it was worth a try, and basically a way to frame my usual talk about what we all should do. Mostly I say, go outdoors and sit and talk to a friend: this is our primate utopia and very easy on the planet.

Your latest work, yet to be published, is about Galileo. Or about the relationship between science and politics. Or is it ambition and religion? Or work and age?

A bit of all those things, but mostly I was thinking science and history; what science is, how it has affected history, how it could in the future. And also about Galileo's actual work, which is ever so interesting. He was a great character.

What's you favorite city?

San Francisco is my favorite city, but I also like New York, London, Edinburgh, Paris, Venice, Sydney, Vancouver, and Kathmandu.

You broke into print the "usual" (old) way for SF writers—through short stories. Do you plan to go back to short fiction? What do you think of today's dwindling story "market?"

I don't rule out going back to short fiction, but I like novels better and that's what I'm focused on; that may never stop. I think it's too bad about the dwindling market and wonder if reading habits are changing with the Internet. In a way shorter fiction should possibly benefit by the quickness of web life, but I don't know. I'm enough outside it not to be thinking about it too much.

SF used to have an agenda—the future, and in particular, space travel. Does it have an agenda today?

I don't know! I think it has to have the agenda of the future. But when the future doesn't include space travel as the obvious next step, it gets a lot more complicated. Things on Earth don't look so science fictional. And yet the whole world in a sense is in a science fiction novel that we write together. So it's all very confusing. My response is to say "just keep writing, one novel at a time" and hope for the best.

Do you think there is life on other planets? Intelligence? Do you think we will even "make contact?"

I do think there is life on other planets, and also intelligence, but what kind of intelligence I think is very mysterious, and making contact will be a serious problem, maybe too much a problem to ever really happen, partly because of the size of the universe (bigger than we think) and also the potentially inexplicable nature of alien intelligence, so that we won't be able to communicate with it (the *Solaris* problem, after Lem's great novel).

How come there is no space travel in Years of Rice and Salt? *Do you think space travel is a Eurocentric enterprise?*

No, I think any technological civilization would think about space travel, because of the moon, and the simplicity of rockets, and so on. I didn't have it in *Years of Rice and Salt* partly by accidental omission, partly because that book only takes history about seventy years past us; and I think without Percival Lowell, we might not have gotten to the moon yet, and might not for another century or so. That was a freak event, with a genealogy that runs from Lowell's fantasia to the novels of Lasswitz/Bogdanov/Wells to the German Rocket Society to von Braun to WWII to NASA. Without all those elements, including Lowell's hallucinations about Mars, we might still not have gotten to the moon. So, in my alternative history, I thought it was okay to leave it out. It would have only gotten a sentence or two anyway if I had thought of it.

BIBLIOGRAPHY

BOOKS

The Wild Shore
    Novel. Locus Poll winner, Best First Novel; Philip K. Dick Award Runner-up.

    a. Ace Books, 1984.
    b. Futura (UK), 1985.
    c. McDonald (UK) 1986.
    d. Bastei (W. Germany), 1986.
    e. Hayakawa (Japan), 1986.
    f. J'ai Lu (France), 1986.
    g. Ediciones Jucar (Spain), 1989.
    h. Interno Giallo (Italy), 1990.
    i. Zysk (Poland), 1998.
    j. HarperCollins (UK), 1997.
    k. Tor Orb, 1997.
    l. Polyaris (Russia).
    m. Laser (Czech Republic).
    n. Minotauro (Spain) 2006.

Icehenge

> Novel.
> a. Ace Books, 1984.
> b. Futura (UK), 1985.
> c. McDonald (UK), 1986.
> d. Denoel (France), 1986.
> e. Editrice Nord (Italy), 1986.
> f. Bastei (W. Germany), 1987.
> g. Tor Books, 1990.
> h. HarperCollins (UK), 1997.
> i. Tor Orb, 1998.
> j. KZ Zagrebacka Naklada (Croatia).
> k. Minotauro (Spain).
> l. Gallimard (France), 2004.

The Novels of Philip K. Dick

> Criticism. (UCSD dissertation)
> a. UMI Research Press, 1984; paperback, 1989.
> b. Chapter 4 reprinted as "Introduction" to Heyne
edition of PKD's *The Man in the High Castle*, Heyne,
2000.
> c. Shayol (Germany) 2005.
> d. Les Moutons Electronique (France), 2005.

The Memory of Whiteness

> Novel.
> a. Tor Books, 1985.
> b. McDonald (UK), 1986.
> c. Futura (UK), 1987.
> d. Bastei (W. Germany), 1987.
> e. J'ai Lu (France), 1987.
> f. Tokyo Sogensha (Japan), 1996
> g. Tor Orb, 1997.
> h. HarperCollins (UK), 1999.

    i. Librarie Generale Francaise, (France).

The Planet on the Table
    Stories. *New York Times* Notable Book.
    a. Tor Books, 1986.
    b. Futura (UK), 1987.
    c. J'ai Lu (France) 1989.
    d. Bastei (W. Germany), 1988.
    e. Editorial Caminho (Portugal), 1989.
    f. Tor Orb (w/Remaking History), 1995.

The Gold Coast
    Novel. John W. Campbell Award runner-up; *New York Times* Notable Book.
    a. Tor Books, 1988.
    b. Futura (UK), 1989.
    c. J'ai Lu (France), 1989.
    d. Hayakawa (Japan), 1991.
    e. Bastei (Germany), 1989.
    f. Ediciones Jucar (Spain), 1990.
    g. Ultramarine Press, 1995.
    h. HarperCollins (UK), 1997.
    i. Tor Orb, 1997.
    j. Akti-Oxi (Greece), 1998.
    k. Polyaris (Russia).
    l. Minotauro (Spain) 2006.

Escape From Kathmandu
    Stories.
    a. Tor Books, 1989.
    b. Unwin-Hyman (UK), 1990.
    c. Grafton (UK), 1991.
    d. Easton Press, 1989.
    e. Bastei (Germany), 1990.

f. Zysk (Poland), 1997.

g. Tor Orb, 1996.

h. AST (Russia).

i. Epos (Slovakia).

j. Heyne (Germany), 2001.

Pacific Edge
Novel. John W. Campbell Award winner, Best Novel; *New York Times* Notable Book.

a. Tor Books, 1990.

b. "Oh See" (from Chapter One) *The Los Angeles Times*, May 1989.

c. Unwin-Hyman (UK), 1990.

d. Grafton (UK), 1991.

e. Easton Press, 1990.

f. Bastei (Germany), 1992.

g. HarperCollins, 1997.

h. Tor Orb, 1997.

i. Polyaris (Russia).

j. Minotauro (Spain).

A Short, Sharp Shock
Novella. Locus Award winner, Best Novella.

a. Zeising Books, 1990.

b. Tor Double no. 23, 1990.

c. *Asimov's Science Fiction Magazine Magazine*, November 1990.

d. Bantam Books, 1995.

e. HarperCollins (UK), 2000.

f. US Audio Book.

Remaking History
Stories.

a. Tor Books, 1991.

b. J'ai Lu, 1991.

c. HarperCollins (UK), selection as "Down and Out in the Year 2000," 1992.

d. Tor Orb (w/Planet On the Table), 1995.

e. HarperCollins (UK), selection as "Vinland the Dream," 2002.

Red Mars

Novel. British Science Fiction Award winner; Nebula Award winner; Seiun Award winner (Japan).

a. HarperCollins, 1992.

b. Bantam Books, 1993.

c. Bruna (Holland), 1993.

d. Heyne (Germany), 1997.

e. Easton Press, 1993.

f. Minotauro (Spain), 1995, 2007.

g. Presse de la Cite (France), 1994.

h. Interno Giallo (Italy), 1995.

i. Prosznyski (Poland), 1997.

j. Nemira (Romania), 1997, 2008.

k. Opus (Israel), 1998.

l. Izvori (Croatia), 1997.

m. Faces Publishing (Taiwan), 2000.

n. Bard (Bulgaria).

o. N & N Kiado (Hungary).

p. Tokyo Sogensha (Japan), 1998.

q. Polyaris (Russia).

r. Si Chuan Science and Technology (China).

s. Meia Sete (Brazil).

t. Recorded Books, Inc. (audio), 2000.

u. Vita Breva (Greece), 2000.

v. Kabalci Yayinevi (Turkey).

w. Moc Knjige (Serbia).

x. Banshies sro (Czech Republic).

y. combined edition, *Red Green and Blue*, Omnibus (France), 2006.

z. Beijing Hongwenguan (mainland China).

Green Mars

Novel. Hugo Award winner; Locus Award winner; Ignotus Award winner (Spain); Gigamesh Award winner (Spain).

a. HarperCollins, 1994.

b. Bantam Books, 1994.

c. Heyne (Germany), 1998.

d. Minotauro (Spain), 1997.

e. Presse de la Cite (France), 1996.

f. Nemira (Romania), 1997.

g. Proscynski (Poland), 1999.

h. Bruna (Holland), 1998.

i. N & N Kiado (Hungary).

j. Bard (Bulgaria).

k. Izvori (Croatia).

l. Polyaris (Russia).

m. Opus (Israel), 1999.

n. Faces Publishing (Taiwan), 2001.

o. Tokyo Sogensha (Japan), 2002.

p. Si Chuan Science And Technology (China).

q. Meia Sete (Brazil).

r. Recorded Books, Inc. (audio), 2001.

s. Kabalci Yayinevi (Turkey).

t. Easton Press, 2001.

u. Moc Knjige (Serbia).

v. Banshies sro (Czech Republic).

w. Beijing Hongweguan (mainland China)

Blue Mars

Novel. Hugo Award winner; Locus Award winner; Ozone Poll winner (France); *New York Times* Notable Book.

 a. HarperCollins, 1996.
 b. Bantam Books, 1996.
 c. Heyne (Germany), 1999.
 d. Presse de la Cite (France), 1997.
 e. Minotauro (Spain), 1998.
 f. Nemira (Romania), 2000.
 g. Bard (Bulgaria).
 h. Polyaris (Russia).
 i. Opus (Israel), 2001.
 j. Faces Publishing (Taiwan), 2001.
 k. Tokyo Sogensha (Japan).
 l. Easton Press, 1996.
 m. Proszynski (Poland), 2000.
 n. Si Chuan Science And Technology (China).
 o. Meia Sete (Brazil).
 p. Recorded Books, Inc. (audio).
 q. Kabalci Yayinevi (Turkey).
 r. Izvori (Croatia).
 s. Moc Knjige (Serbia).
 t. Beijing Hongwenguan (mainland China).

Antarctica

 Novel. Alex Award winner (American Library Association); *New York Times* Notable Book.

 a. HarperCollins, 1997.
 b. Bantam Books, 1998.
 c. Presse de la Cite (France), 1998.
 d. Heyne (Germany).
 e. Kodansha (Japan), 2004.
 f. Minotauro (Spain), 1999.
 g. Cicero (Denmark), 1999.
 h. Otava (Finland), 2000.

i. Easton Press, 1998.

j. Proszynski (Poland), 1999.

k. Books On Tape (US Audio).

l. Libre Expression (Quebec), 1999.

m. Excerpt in *The Ends of the Earth*, ed. Elizabeth Kolbert and Francis Spufford, Bloomsbury Books, 2007.

The Martians

Stories. Locus Award winner, Best Collection.

a. HarperCollins, 1999.

b. Bantam Books, 1999.

c. Easton Press, 1999.

d. Presse de la Cite (France), 2000.

e. Heyne (Germany), 2002.

f. Minotauro (Spain), 2004.

g. Kabalci (Turkey).

The Years of Rice and Salt

Novel. Locus Award winner, Best Science Fiction Novel.

a. Bantam, 2002.

b. HarperCollins (UK), 2002.

c. Easton Press, 2002.

d. Presse de la Cite (France), 2003, 2006.

e. Yolimwon (Korea), 2007.

f. Minotauro (Spain), 2003.

g. Izvori (Croatia), 2004.

h. Kabalci (Turkey).

i. Ulpius-haz, (Hungary).

j. Dolnoslaskie (Poland).

k. Newton Compton (Italy), 2007.

l. Shanghai Sanhui (China).

Forty Signs of Rain
　　Novel. Alex Award, American Library Association.
　　　　a. Bantam, 2004.
　　　　b. HarperCollins (UK), 2004.
　　　　c. Easton Press, 2004.
　　　　d. Minotauro (Spain), 2005.
　　　　e. Presse de la Cite (France), 2006.
　　　　f. Tritonic (Romania).
　　　　g. Bruna (Holland), 2006.
　　　　h. Audible.com (audio).
　　　　i. Resif Yayincilik (Turkey).

Fifty Degrees Below
　　Novel. Alex Award, American Library Association.
　　　　a. Bantam, 2005.
　　　　b. HarperCollins (UK), 2005.
　　　　c. Minotauro (Spain).
　　　　d. Tritonic (Romania).
　　　　e. Easton Press, 2000.
　　　　f. Presse de al Cite (France), 2008.
　　　　g. Bruno (Holland), 2007.
　　　　h. Audible.com (audio).
　　　　i. Resif Yayincilik (Turkey).

Sixty Days and Counting
　　Novel.
　　　　a. Bantam, 2007.
　　　　b. HarperCollins (UK), 2007.
　　　　c. Minotauro (Spain).
　　　　d. Bruno (Holland), 2008.
　　　　e. Easton Press, 2007.
　　　　f. Presse de la Cite (France).

g. Audible.com (audio).
h. Resif Yayincilik (Turkey).

Galileo's Dream
      Novel.
      a. Bantam, 2009.
      b. HarperCollins (UK), 2009.

STORIES

"In Pierson's Orchestra"
      Orbit 18, ed. Damon Knight, Harper and Row, 1976.

"Coming Back to Dixieland"
      Orbit 18, ed. Damon Knight, Harper and Row, 1976.

"The Thing Itself"
      Clarion SF, ed. Kate Wilhelm, Berkley Books, 1976.

"The Disguise"
      Orbit 19, ed. Damon Knight, Harper and Row, 1977.

"On the North Pole of Pluto"
      Orbit 21, ed. Damon Knight, Harper and Row, 1980.

"Venice Drowned"
      Nebula Award nominee.
      Universe 11, ed. Terry Carr, Doubleday, 1981.

"Exploring Fossil Canyon"

Universe 12, ed. Terry Carr, Doubleday, 1982.

"To Leave a Mark"
    Hugo Award nominee.
    The Magazine of Fantasy and Science Fiction, November 1982.

"Black Air"
    World Fantasy Award winner, Best Novella; Hugo Award nominee; Nebula Award nominee.
    The Magazine of Fantasy and Science Fiction, March 1983.

"Stone Eggs"
    Universe 13, ed. Terry Carr, Doubleday, 1983.

"Ridge Running"
    Hugo Award nominee.
    The Magazine of Fantasy and Science Fiction, January 1984.

"The Lucky Strike"
    Nebula Award nominee; Hugo Award nominee
    Universe 14, ed. Terry Carr, Doubleday, 1984.

Green Mars
    Novella. Nebula Award nominee; Hugo Award nominee.
    Asimov's Science Fiction Magazine, September 1985.

"Mercurial"
    Universe 15, ed. Terry Carr, Doubleday, 1985.

"Down and Out in the Year 2000"
    Asimov's Science Fiction Magazine, April 1986.

"A Transect"
The Magazine of Fantasy and Science Fiction, May 1986.

Escape From Kathmandu
Novella. Nebula Award nominee; Hugo Award nominee.
Asimov's Science Fiction Magazine, September 1986.

"Our Town"
Omni, November 1986.

"The Blind Geometer"
Nebula Award winner; Hugo Award nominee.
Asimov's Science Fiction Magazine, August 1987.

"The Return From Rainbow Bridge"
The Magazine of Fantasy and Science Fiction, August 1987.

"Mother Goddess of the World"
Asimov's Poll winner; Hugo Award nominee.
Asimov's Science Fiction Magazine, October 1987.

"The Man In the Mirror"
Foundation (UK), Winter 1987.

"The Memorial"
In the Field of Fire, ed. Jack and Jeanne Dann, Tor Books, 1987.

"Glacier"
Asimov's Science Fiction Magazine, September 1988.

"The Lunatics"

Asimov's Science Fiction Magazine, mid-December 1988.
"Before I Wake"
Nebula Award nominee.
Interzone no. 27, Jan/Feb 1989.

"The True Nature of Shangri-La"
Asimov's Science Fiction Magazine, December 1989.

"The Kingdom Underground"
Escape From Kathmandu, Tor 1989.

"The Part of Us That Loves"
Full Spectrum II, ed. Lou Aronica et al, Bantam
Books, 1989.

"Remaking History"
What Might Have Been, ed. Gregory Benford,
Bantam Books 1989.

"Zurich"
The Magazine of Fantasy and Science Fiction,
March 1990.

"Muir On Shasta"
A Sensitive Dependence on Initial Conditions, Pulphouse Press, 1990.

"A History of the Twentieth Century, With Illustra-
tions"
Asimov's Science Fiction Magazine, April 1991.

"The Translator"
*Universe On*e, ed. Robert Silverberg and Karen
Haber, Doubleday, 1990.

"Vinland the Dream"

Nebula Award nominee.
Alternate Americas, ed. Gergory Benford, Tor Books, 1992.

"Sexual Dimorphism"
Asimov's Science Fiction Magazine, June 1999.

"Arthur Sternbach Brings the Curveball to Mars"
Asimov's Science Fiction Magazine, September 1999.

"A Martian Romance"
Asimov's Science Fiction Magazine, October/November 1999.

"Review: Science in the Third Millennium"
Nature, January 6, 2000.

"UCSD and Permaculture, a Science Fiction Story"
Perspectives, UCSD alumni magazine, excerpts.

"Prometheus Unbound, At Last, and None Too Soon"
Nature, June 2005.

ABOUT THE AUTHOR

Kim Stanley Robinson (b. 1952) was raised in Orange County, California, and despite obtaining a PhD in literature (UC San Diego) has been a successful novelist since the early 1980s. Describing himself as a "green socialist," he is one of today's most prominent SF authors, and along with his friend Ursula LeGuin, one of the most consistently radical in humanist outlook and literary practice. His newest work is *Galileo's Dream*.

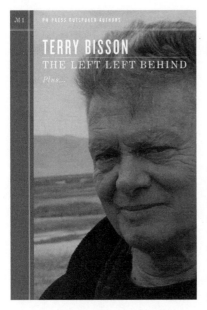

PM PRESS
OUTSPOKEN AUTHORS

The Left Left Behind
Terry Bisson
978-1-60486-086-3
$12

Hugo and Nebula award-winner Terry Bisson is best known for his short stories, which range from the southern sweetness of "Bears Discover Fire" to the alienated aliens of "They're Made out of Meat." He is also a 1960s' New Left vet with a history of activism and an intact (if battered) radical ideology.

The *Left Behind* novels (about the so-called "Rapture" in which all the born-agains ascend straight to heaven) are among the bestselling Christian books in the US, describing in lurid detail the adventures of those "left behind" to battle the Anti-Christ. Put Bisson and the Born-Agains together, and what do you get? *The Left Left Behind*—a sardonic, merciless, tasteless, take-no-prisoners satire of the entire apocalyptic enterprise that spares no one-predatory preachers, goth lingerie, Pacifica radio, Indian casinos, gangsta rap, and even "art cars" at Burning Man.

Plus: "Special Relativity," a one-act drama that answers the question: When Albert Einstein, Paul Robeson, J. Edgar Hoover are raised from the dead at an anti-Bush rally, which one wears the dress? As with all Outspoken Author books, there is a deep interview and autobiography: at length, in-depth, no-holds-barred and all-bets off: an extended tour though the mind and work, the history and politics of our Outspoken Author. Surprises are promised.

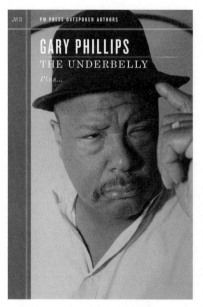

PM PRESS
OUTSPOKEN AUTHORS

The Underbelly
Gary Phillips
978-1-60486-206-5
$12

The explosion of wealth and development in downtown L.A. is a thing of wonder. But regardless of how big and shiny our buildings get, we should not forget the ones this wealth and development has overlooked and pushed out. This is the context for Phillips' novella *The Underbelly*, as a semi-homeless Vietnam vet named Magrady searches for a wheelchair-bound friend gone missing from Skid Row - a friend who might be working a dangerous scheme against major players. Magrady's journey is a solo sortie in which the flashback-prone protagonist must deal with the impact of gentrification; take-no-prisoners community organizers; an unflinching cop from his past in Vietnam; an elderly sexpot out for his bones; a lusted-after magical skull; chronic-lovin' knuckleheads; and the perils of chili cheese fries at midnight. Combining action, humor and a street level gritty POV, *Underbelly* is illustrated with photos and drawings.

Plus: a rollicking interview wherein Phillips riffs on Ghetto Lit, politics, noir and the proletariat, the good negroes and bad knee-grows of pop culture, Redd Foxx and Lord Buckley, and wrestles with the future of books in the age of want.

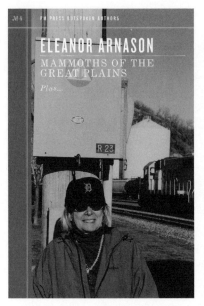

PM PRESS
OUTSPOKEN AUTHORS

*Mammoths of the
Great Plains*
Eleanor Arnason
978-1-60486-075-7
$12

When President Thomas Jefferson sent Lewis and Clark to explore the West, he told them to look especially for mammoths. Jefferson had seen bones and tusks of the great beasts in Virginia, and he suspected—he hoped!—that they might still roam the Great Plains. In Eleanor Arnason's imaginative alternate history, they do: shaggy herds thunder over the grasslands, living symbols of the oncoming struggle between the Native peoples and the European invaders. And in an unforgettable saga that soars from the badlands of the Dakotas to the icy wastes of Siberia, from the Russian Revolution to the American Indian Movement protests of the 1960s, Arnason tells of a modern woman's struggle to use the weapons of DNA science to fulfill the ancient promises of her Lakota heritage.

Plus: "Writing During World War Three," a politically un-correct take on multiculturalism from an SF point-of-view; and an Outspoken Interview that takes you straight into the heart and mind of one of today's edgiest and most uncompromising speculative authors.

FRIENDS OF

In the year since its founding – and on a mere shoestring – PM Press has risen to the formidable challenge of publishing and distributing knowledge and entertainment for the struggles ahead. With over 40 releases in 2009, we have published an impressive and stimulating array of literature, art, music, politics, and culture. Using every available medium, we've succeeded in connecting those hungry for ideas and information to those putting them into practice.

Friends of PM allows you to directly help impact, amplify, and revitalize the discourse and actions of radical writers, filmmakers, and artists. It provides us with a stable foundation from which we can build upon our early successes and provides a much-needed subsidy for the materials that can't necessarily pay their own way. You can help make that happen—and receive every new title automatically delivered to your door once a month—by joining as a Friend of PM Press. Here are your options:

    • $25 a month: Get all books and pamphlets plus 50% discount on all webstore purchases.

    • $25 a month: Get all CDs and DVDs plus 50% discount on all webstore purchases.

    • $40 a month: Get all PM Press releases plus 50% discount on all webstore purchases

    • $100 a month: Sustainer. - Everything plus PM merchandise, free downloads, and 50% discount on all webstore purchases.

Just go to **WWW.PMPRESS.ORG** to sign up. Your card will be billed once a month, until you tell us to stop. Or until our efforts succeed in bringing the revolution around. Or the financial meltdown of Capital makes plastic redundant. Whichever comes first.

PM Press was founded at the end of 2007 by a small collection of folks with decades of publishing, media, and organizing experience. PM co-founder Ramsey Kanaan started AK Press as a young teenager in Scotland almost 30 years ago and, together with his fellow PM Press coconspirators, has published and distributed hundreds of books, pamphlets, CDs, and DVDs. Members of PM have founded enduring book fairs, spearheaded victorious tenant organizing campaigns, and worked closely with bookstores, academic conferences, and even rock bands to deliver political and challenging ideas to all walks of life. We're old enough to know what we're doing and young enough to know what's at stake.

We seek to create radical and stimulating fiction and nonfiction books, pamphlets, t-shirts, visual and audio materials to entertain, educate and inspire you. We aim to distribute these through every available channel with every available technology - whether that means you are seeing anarchist classics at our bookfair stalls; reading our latest vegan cookbook at the café; downloading geeky fiction e-books; or digging new music and timely videos from our website.

PM Press is always on the lookout for talented and skilled volunteers, artists, activists and writers to work with. If you have a great idea for a project or can contribute in some way, please get in touch.

PM Press
PO Box 23912
Oakland CA 94623
510-658-3906
www.pmpress.org